Is there anyth   y?

How

New York
Vicki Lewis Thompson is back in the Blaze lineup
for 2013, and this year she's
offering her readers *even more*....

Sons of Chance

*Chance isn't just the last name of these
rugged Wyoming cowboys—it's their motto, too!*

Saddle up with

#751 *I CROSS MY HEART*
(June)

#755 *WILD AT HEART*
(July)

#759 *THE HEART WON'T LIE*
(August)

And the first full-length
Sons of Chance Christmas story

#775 *COWBOYS & ANGELS*
(December)

Take a chance...on a Chance!

Dear Reader,

For those of you who've stuck with me through all twelve books (and more to come!) in the Sons of Chance series, I have a special treat for you in this story. In addition to a smokin' hot love affair between Western writer Michael Hartford and housekeeper Keri Fitzpatrick, you'll celebrate Sarah Chance's wedding to Pete Beckett. When I began the series in 2010, Sarah was grieving her late husband. Now, three years later, she's starting a new life with Pete! Awwww.

If you're joining me for the first time, I promise that you won't get lost while reading *The Heart Won't Lie*. I work hard to make sure that someone who's just discovered the series can enjoy the book without having read the previous eleven. I invite you to dive right into Michael and Keri's story, which was fun for me because Michael's an author, and I do know the breed. Combining the sensibilities of a writer with the hotness of a cowboy created serious sizzle!

Also, don't forget that this year I'll have a Christmas-themed Sons of Chance book! Look for *Cowboys & Angels* toward the end of November. I predict it'll be a white Christmas at the Last Chance Ranch, and I'd love to see you all there. In the meantime, here are Michael and Keri!

Sizzlingly yours,

Vicki Lewis Thompson

Vicki Lewis Thompson

The Heart Won't Lie

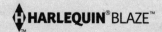

Recycling programs
for this product may
not exist in your area.

ISBN-13: 978-0-373-79763-9

THE HEART WON'T LIE

Copyright © 2013 by Vicki Lewis Thompson

Printed in U.S.A.

ABOUT THE AUTHOR

New York Times bestselling author Vicki Lewis Thompson's love affair with cowboys started with the Lone Ranger, continued through Maverick and took a turn south of the border with Zorro. She views cowboys as the Western version of knights in shining armor—rugged men who value honor, honesty and hard work. Fortunately for her, she lives in the Arizona desert, where broad-shouldered, lean-hipped cowboys abound. Blessed with such an abundance of inspiration, she only hopes that she can do them justice. Visit her website, www.vickilewisthompson.com.

Books by Vicki Lewis Thompson

To get the inside scoop on Harlequin Blaze and its talented writers, be sure to check out blazeauthors.com.

Other titles by this author available in ebook format.
Don't miss any of our special offers. Write to us at the following address for information on our newest releases.

Harlequin Reader Service
U.S.: 3010 Walden Ave., P.O. Box 1325, Buffalo, NY 14269
Canadian: P.O. Box 609, Fort Erie, Ont. L2A 5X3

To Louis L'Amour, an author who claimed that, if necessary, he could write a story sitting in the median of a busy intersection. He's my kind of guy!

Prologue

August 13, 1988, from the diary of Eleanor Chance

MY GRANDSON JACK, who turns ten this fall, can be a trial at times. I cut him some slack because he still carries the scars from being abandoned by his mother when he was a toddler. I'm not sure if that wound is ever going to heal, no matter how much love we all give him.

Truth be told, Jack and I have a special bond because I took over raising him for a couple of years until my son Jonathon married his second wife, Sarah. I've stepped back now, because Sarah is terrific with Jack and the two sons who came along after that, Nick and Gabe. The Last Chance Ranch is a happier place with Sarah living here.

But Jack is still a handful. Even so, he'll always have a special place in my heart, and that's partly because we both love to read, especially Westerns. Whenever the real world gets too complicated for Jack, he escapes into a book. I just introduced him to one of my favorites, Louis L'Amour, and he's gobbling up those stories.

I remember doing the same when I first discovered

Louis L'Amour back in the fifties. That man could spin a yarn like nobody's business. I was so sad to hear that he'd died this past June, but he left us a whole lot of good reading, and I'm grateful for that.

Winters are dark and cold in Jackson Hole, and I don't know what I'd do without my Westerns. You can bet this winter both Jack and I will be curled up in front of the fire with a book. I envy Jack having all those Louis L'Amour stories ahead of him.

I may read them all again, myself. I should probably try one of the new authors, like that Larry McMurtry everyone's so keen on. But it just seems as if nobody quite comes up to Louis L'Amour.

1

Present day

"WHAT NAME DO you want to go by while you're at the ranch?"

Michael James Hartford, aka Western writer Jim Ford, thought about how to answer Jack Chance, who was currently driving him to the Last Chance Ranch. Michael had flown to Wyoming from New York City so he could learn some cowboy basics before a publicity team put him in front of a video camera in three weeks. Nobody besides Jack was supposed to know Michael was also Jim Ford, who wrote as if he could ride and rope but…couldn't.

He wondered if he should be known as Mike while he was here. A shortened name seemed better for a cowboy, but he already had his Jim Ford persona. If he adopted too many alternate names he wouldn't remember which one he should answer to. "Michael's fine," he said. "Michael Hartford. That shouldn't tip anybody off."

"Michael Hartford it is, then. I don't think you have

anything to worry about, though. Some of the hands have read your books, but they'd never believe a greenhorn like you could possibly be the guy who writes those stories."

"Yeah, I know." Michael took the blow to his ego with good humor. His lack of cowboying skills really was an embarrassing joke.

"Besides, the picture in the back of your books shows you with a mustache. That really changes how a guy looks."

"I grow that mustache before I have to make any appearances or get my picture taken. Then I shave it off. I'll have to start growing it again next week. Between that and the Stetson, I've fooled just about everybody except my family, and they're not about to broadcast the fact that I'm Jim Ford."

"I don't get that. You'd think they'd be proud of you."

Michael laughed. "They would be if I wrote deep, philosophical literature. The Hartfords are old money, loaded to the gills with culture. They don't want to claim a pulp fiction author. That's actually worked to my advantage. If nobody knows who Jim Ford really is, then nobody knows that he's never been on a horse in his life."

"That still boggles my mind. You write as if you're a real cowboy. I would have sworn you'd done all those things. What's your secret?"

"Research." Michael felt good knowing he'd managed to get it right, despite his lack of experience. "Plus I grew up reading Louis L'Amour."

"Me, too. I didn't think I'd find his equal, but you've

hooked me real good. I wish my grandmother was still alive. She would have loved your books, too."

"Thank you. That's high praise."

"I mean it sincerely." Jack shook his head. "But I can't figure you out. The way you write, I can tell you love the idea of being a cowboy. How come you never got the itch to spend time on a ranch?"

"You hit the nail on the head. I love the *idea* of being a cowboy, but I've avoided the reality, in case it doesn't live up to my image of it." *Or I don't.* "I'm selling a fantasy, and if I discover that fantasy doesn't exist…"

"Damnation. You mean this visit could burst your bubble? I don't want that on my conscience."

"Hey, Jack, you're not the one forcing me into this. The publicity department is to blame." He blew out a breath. "No, that's not right, either. I created this stupid situation all on my own. I chose to write about a world I don't know firsthand, and then I accidentally became a big success at it."

Jack nodded. "I noticed. Your name keeps getting bigger on the cover."

"If my books weren't selling so well the publisher would never pay for a video of me playing cowboy. My secret would be safe. But they made it clear I need to do this video if I expect continued support from the marketing team."

Smiling, Jack glanced over at him. "Cheer up, little buckaroo. It won't be so bad."

"Easy for you to say. I'm going to make a damned fool of myself, and you know it."

"Maybe so, but I'll be the only one who'll know it. Your lessons will be as private as I can make them."

"Thank you for that." Michael relaxed a little. "Bethany told me I could trust you." He'd met motivational author Bethany Grace on the Opal Knightly TV talk show and they'd kept in touch. When he'd needed riding lessons on the QT he'd thought of her, because she'd grown up in Jackson Hole.

"Bethany's good people," Jack said. "Did you catch her wedding to Nash Bledsoe on Opal's show?"

"Sure did. Nash is a friend of yours, right?"

"Yep." Jack checked his mirrors before pulling around a slow-moving semi. "Nash owns a little spread next door to the Last Chance."

"Bethany mentioned that. She inherited it, sold it to Nash and the rest reads like a romance novel."

Jack chuckled. "It does, at that. Poor Nash, though, having to get hitched on national TV. There was some talk of me being the best man at that shindig, but it was way better for Nash's dad to have that honor."

Michael was beginning to get a bead on Jack's personality so he made a calculated guess. "You didn't want to do it, did you?"

"*Hell,* no. Not after I found out I had to wear *makeup.*" Jack grimaced.

"It's not so bad, little buckaroo."

"Maybe not for a city slicker like yourself, but real cowboys don't wear makeup."

"What about your friend Nash? I guarantee he had on makeup during that wedding."

"Only because otherwise he wouldn't get to marry Bethany. Bethany was beholden to Opal for letting her out of her TV contract, and Opal was determined to stage that wedding on TV."

"What a guy won't do for love." As he said it, Michael realized he had no personal experience to go by, and that was a damned shame.

"Ain't it the truth. My wife, Josie, has got me wrapped around her little finger. Between her and my kid, Archie, I'm like a bull with a ring in its nose. They can lead me anywhere."

Michael grinned. "I seriously doubt that."

"No, really. They've got me hog-tied. How about you? Is there some citified lady calling the shots in your life?"

"Nope."

"Too busy?"

"Kind of, but that's not really the problem. The high-society women I meet don't interest me, but I can't date the ones I meet as Jim Ford because they think I'm a cowboy, which I'm not." He didn't like being caught between worlds, not belonging in either one, but he hadn't figured out what to do about it. He envied a guy like Jack, who knew who he was and where he fit in.

Jack tapped his fingers against the steering wheel. "But you will be a cowboy."

Michael felt a jolt of pleasure at the possibility. But he had to be realistic. "In a week? Not likely."

"Are you doubting my ability?"

"No, I'm doubting mine."

"Well, cut that out right now. First and foremost, a cowboy faces every challenge with an air of quiet confidence."

"Of course he does, especially if he's a hero in one of my books." Michael looked over at Jack and expected they'd share a laugh over that. Instead, Jack seemed totally serious. "Wait, you're not kidding, are you?"

"No, I'm not. Being a cowboy is a state of mind. You can start working on your attitude before you ever put your booted foot in a stirrup."

"I see." Michael was fascinated. For years he'd assumed that the larger-than-life cowboys in his books didn't exist in reality. But Jack Chance was proving that assumption had been dead wrong.

AFTER A YEAR working as the housekeeper at the Last Chance's main house, Keri Fitzpatrick, former Baltimore socialite, could wield a mean mop. She'd learned the basics from her boss, Sarah Chance, and the cook, Mary Lou Simms. Following their instructions, Keri could clean windows like nobody's business and polish bathroom fixtures until they sparkled like fine silver.

But she'd challenge anybody, even a professional armed with power equipment, to eliminate some mysterious smell left by eight adolescent boys. They'd been part of the Last Chance's summer program for disadvantaged youths, and they'd moved out early that morning. She'd been cleaning nonstop ever since except for a short lunch break with Mary Lou.

The second floor, where the boys had slept in two rooms fitted with bunk beds, was warm, and she dripped with sweat. Putting her hair in a ponytail to get it off her neck hadn't helped cool her off much. She'd opted for jeans instead of shorts because she'd anticipated getting on her hands and knees for this job.

Sure enough, she'd had to clean some gunk off the baseboards. God knew what it was. She'd dealt with this last August right after being hired, but she was sure the previous year's batch of kids hadn't left a stink this bad. She'd noticed a slight odor yesterday, but had thought it would leave with the kids. Instead, it was worse.

Glancing at her watch, she gasped. The wealthy tenderfoot from New York City was due any minute. She'd been told very little about him, but Jack had said the guy was used to the best.

Keri had been raised in luxury, too. Although she didn't live that way now, she knew exactly how to prepare guest quarters for a wealthy man. She'd spit-shined his room, which was at the other end of the hall, right across from her room. The crockery vase of wildflowers she'd placed on his dresser gave off a delicate aroma.

The poor things couldn't begin to compete with the stench coming from the boys' rooms. She'd already tested the situation, and the entire top floor, including the tenderfoot's room, smelled like a garbage dump. Opening all the windows hadn't made a dent in the foul odor.

Desperate to find the source, she went through everything again—closets, drawers, even under the bunk beds. Finally she found a kitchen matchbox crammed so far under one of the bunks that she'd missed it when she'd swept and mopped. Using a broom, she nudged it free and nearly gagged. She'd found her culprit.

She shouldn't have looked, but after all this effort, she wanted to know what was in that box. As she slid open the matchbox, the smell got worse. She stared at a very fragrant, and very dead, mouse. It rested on a carefully folded tissue, and a second tissue covered the lower part of its body, so only the head was exposed.

Guessing what had happened wasn't hard. She'd been around the boys enough to understand how their minds worked. They'd found the dead mouse, decided it deserved a decent burial and put it in the matchbox. Then they'd forgotten all about it.

Now what? She could throw it in the trash, but that seemed wrong. They'd folded the tissues so carefully, and she was touched by their concern for the little creature's final resting place. Silly as it seemed, she wanted to bury it the way they'd intended.

Okay, so she would. Holding the box, she walked into the hall. She didn't dare take the smelly thing down the back stairs and through Mary Lou's pristine kitchen, so she made for the curved stairway leading to the front door. If she was very lucky she could get rid of the dead mouse before the tenderfoot arrived.

Luck was not on her side. The front door opened and Jack Chance ushered a broad-shouldered man through it. From this angle he didn't look like a tenderfoot. His jeans were slightly worn and his blue chambray shirt was faded. His leather suitcase was scuffed up some, and even his hat seemed broken in. If she didn't know better, she'd think this was a seasoned cowboy, and a nicely built one, at that.

Jack closed the door behind them. "I'll take you straight upstairs so you can get settled in before dinner."

As Keri froze in position, unsure whether to go up or down, Jack spotted her. "Ah, Keri! Perfect! You can show Michael to his room. Michael Hartford, this is Keri Fitzpatrick, our housekeeper. I'm sure she has your room all ready."

Michael Hartford glanced up. "Nice to meet you, Keri."

"Nice to meet you, too." Whoa. Cute guy. Square jaw, strong nose and dreamy eyes that were an unusual blue-gray color. He looked vaguely familiar, too, although she was sure she didn't know anybody named Michael Hartford.

She'd love to show him to his room, but not while she was holding an extremely dead mouse. "Um, Jack, before I show Mr. Hartford to his room, I need to—"

"What's that godawful smell?" Jack wrinkled his nose.

"I found a dead mouse under one of the bunks."

"It's in that box?"

"Yes, and I—"

"Let me have it." Jack started up the stairs. "I'll throw it in the trash."

Although it might not be wise to disagree with the man who signed her paycheck, Keri couldn't let him take the mouse. "That's okay. I'm going to bury it out back. I won't be a minute. The guest room is all ready." She started down the stairs.

"You're going to do *what?*" Blocking her passage, Jack shoved his hat back with his thumb as he stared up at her.

She paused on the step above him. "Bury it." Jack could be intimidating, but she'd also seen him melt whenever he was with Archie, his little son. Jack had marshmallow insides. "The boys fixed it up with tissues and everything, like it was in a little coffin."

Jack's mouth twitched and amusement flickered in his dark eyes. "Keri, those boys are gone. They'll never know what happened to the mouse. Besides, they obviously forgot all about this burial they'd planned."

"I realize that, but it was a sweet impulse, a sign they cared for this little creature. I think it proves that they made progress while they were here, and I'd like to carry out their wishes."

"Or else it was meant as a joke."

"I prefer to believe it was sincere."

"All righty, then." Jack moved aside to let her pass. "Bury it deep. Put a few stones on top. That thing stinks to high heaven and I don't want the dogs digging it up."

"I'll dig a deep hole." She gave their visitor a quick smile as she walked past him. "Welcome to the Last Chance Ranch, Mr. Hartford. Sorry about the dead mouse."

He smiled back. "May it rest in peace."

"That's the idea." She held his gaze for a little longer than was polite, but he had such beautiful eyes, especially when they were lit up with that warm smile of his. She hoped he wouldn't always associate meeting her with the smell of dead animals.

2

AFTER HIS INTRODUCTION to Keri Fitzpatrick, Michael decided he was going to like it here. Most women he knew would refuse to deal with a dead rodent, and if forced to do so, would grab the first opportunity to get rid of it. Instead, Keri had held on to the stinky mouse because she respected the impulse that had caused someone to tuck it into a matchbox.

He would have admired her spunky behavior whether she'd been pretty or not, but she *was* pretty, which made the encounter even better. He'd thoroughly enjoyed those few seconds of gazing into her vivid green eyes. The fact that she was flushed and sweaty made her eyes even brighter and her dark hair more tempting as it escaped from her ponytail and curled damply at her neck.

Her disheveled state probably wasn't her favorite way to greet visitors, but she hadn't bothered to apologize for how she looked. She'd only been concerned about the foul smell of a decaying animal. Good thing he didn't have a weak stomach.

"Sorry about that," Jack said. "Ready to go up?"

"You bet." Michael wanted to ask about Keri. The

scene with the dead mouse had charmed him, and when she'd spoken he'd heard a familiar accent. She was from back east somewhere. Not New York, but close.

He'd felt an instant attraction, and her steady gaze had told him she'd been drawn to him, too. But he didn't ask Jack about her, because that would imply he was intrigued. Maybe he was, but he was here to learn riding and roping skills, not romance the housekeeper.

Pursuing her would be a rotten way to repay the Last Chance's generous hospitality. Besides, it would be totally out of character for him. He wasn't a sexual opportunist, ready to make a move on any good-looking woman he ran across.

"The smell should fade in a bit," Jack said. "At least you'll be at the other end of the hall. The boys stayed down there." He gestured to his right as he topped the stairs. "It'll be a lot more peaceful up here now that they're gone."

"Will you miss them?"

Jack glanced at him. "Interesting that you should ask. I will miss those varmints. When they're here, I'm ready to tear my hair out, but when they leave, the place seems too quiet."

"I can imagine. All that energy must grow on you." Michael was impressed by what he'd heard of the program, which Jack had casually described during the ride from the airport.

Judging from the offhand way Jack had talked about it, he'd only intended to give Michael some background in case the subject came up while he was at the ranch. But Michael had made a mental note to donate to the cause. Jack had refused to charge anything for this week because he claimed it was an honor to tutor his favorite living author. So Michael would reimburse Jack in a different way, one the cowboy couldn't refuse.

"We had to shovel them out of here, though," Jack said, "to make room for wedding guests arriving at the end of the week."

"Right. The wedding." Bethany had told Michael that Sarah, the ranch's matriarch, was marrying Peter Beckett. Sarah had been widowed several years ago, and everyone seemed thrilled that she'd fallen in love again. "I'm still worried that I'm here at a bad time."

"No, you're here at a good time." Jack grinned as they headed down the hall. "Much as I love my mother and respect Pete, I hate all the fuss and bother that goes into the planning stages of a wedding. You're the perfect excuse to get me out of that. Come Saturday I'll dress up and play my role, but until then I'm busy with an important pupil."

Michael had an uneasy moment. "Why am I so important? I thought nobody knows who I am."

"Don't worry. They don't. But you're Bethany's friend. Nash is like family, and Bethany married Nash, so now Bethany's like family, too. So any friend of Bethany's is a friend of ours."

"I see." Apparently the right connections mattered in the West just as they mattered back east.

"Here's your room. Used to be mine before I got married, but the furniture's all different." Jack walked through a door on the left side of the hallway.

Michael followed him into a large room decorated in shades of green. He noticed a king-size bed and a spectacular view of the Grand Tetons. The jagged peaks still had a smattering of snow, even in August. "Very nice."

"I like it. Looks like Keri picked you some wild-flowers."

Michael had been captured by the view of the mountains, but now he noticed that a bouquet of Indian paint-brush and purple lupine sat on the dresser. "That was thoughtful." Research for his books had taught him what they were, because he wouldn't have had a clue otherwise.

"Yeah, Keri's a gem. She thinks of those things. Don't look for an attached bath, though. The bathroom's right next door, but connecting it would be tricky. The bathtub would get in the way of cutting a door between the rooms. I doubt you're used to walking out into the hall, but it can't be helped."

"Jack, the view from the window is spectacular. I couldn't care less about an attached bath."

"Good." Jack seemed pleased by that. "I'll leave you to unpack, then. Dinner's at six, but you can explore the place before then if you want. I have some issues to handle, but Keri should be back from the mouse funeral soon. If you need a guide, I'm sure she'd be glad to show you around."

"Great." Michael was careful not to sound too eager about having Keri do him that favor. "And thanks, Jack."

"Don't thank me yet. Tomorrow, when your butt's sore from spending hours on a horse and you ache all over, you may not be so thankful."

"I thought you said it wouldn't be too bad?"

Jack smiled. "I didn't want you to panic." Then he turned on his booted heel and left the room.

Some exit line. And thanks to that line, anxiety had him firmly in its grip. What the hell did he think he was doing? Nobody could learn to be a cowboy in a week.

Despite the help from Jack, he could end up falling off his horse during the shooting of the video. That would be embarrassing as hell, both to him and to the publicist. He should have confessed his shortcomings to the gung-ho woman who'd called him with feverish excitement to propose the video they would shoot in three weeks.

Michael could have told her the truth and suggested they drop the idea. Some still shots might work if they found a docile horse for him. But no, he hadn't said those things because he'd wanted to preserve the mystique. Ego, pure and simple.

With a sigh, he walked over to the window and looked out at the majestic Tetons. He should have come to this part of the country years ago. A summer on a dude ranch would have given him what he needed and he wouldn't be in this fix now.

But he hadn't admitted all his fears to Jack. He was deathly afraid that he wouldn't have any talent for being a cowboy, no matter how long he worked at it. By cramming his lessons into a week, he could excuse himself if he failed. If he'd taken an entire summer and failed, he'd have been forced to conclude that he wasn't cut out for the life he wrote about so convincingly.

That would be a tough pill to swallow. He wasn't sure how that would affect his writing, but he had a hunch it would make a dramatic difference. If he'd never tried to be a real cowboy, then he could hang on to the illusion that such a thing might be possible.

"Mr. Hartford?"

He turned from the window and discovered Keri standing in the doorway. "Call me Michael, okay?"

"All right, if that's what you'd prefer. Is there anything you need? I ducked out on my job, but I'm available now."

"Has the mouse received a decent burial?"

"It was quick, but I think the boys would have been satisfied." She studied him. "It's the strangest thing, but I feel as if I know you from somewhere. I don't, do I?"

He didn't dare ask if she read Westerns, but this was the very thing he'd worried about. "I doubt it. I have one of those faces. People often think they know me."

"Maybe, but I've seen you somewhere. I'll figure it out."

That settled one thing for sure. He wouldn't start growing his mustache while he was here.

"So, is everything to your liking? Have you checked out the towel supply in the bathroom?"

"I'm sure it's fine." He still couldn't quite place her accent.

"What's your pillow preference? You currently have down, but I can substitute polyester fill if you're allergic."

"Not allergic. I'm pretty low maintenance." He had a feeling she was, too. She'd hurried right back without stopping to primp.

"Then I'll quit pestering you and let you settle in. If there's anything you need, my room's right across the hall."

"It is?"

"I know. It's not the usual thing to have the employees stay on the same floor as the guests, but Sarah never planned on having more help than Mary Lou, the cook. Then the boys came, which made extra work. When they hired me last summer, they put me up here."

"Do we…uh…share a bathroom?" That could get quite cozy.

"No, we don't. That one is all yours. Last fall Jack renovated my space and installed a small bathroom. He also put one in between the boys' rooms, but it's tiny, too. The nicest one is yours." She backed toward the door. "Let me know if you need anything, though. Seriously."

"Jack said you might give me a tour of the house."

"He did?" She glanced down at her clothes. Without saying a word, she'd managed to communicate her desperate hope for a shower and change of outfit.

"But it can wait until you get cleaned up."

Relief showed in her green eyes. "Thank you. I feel gross. Give me fifteen minutes."

"I'll give you thirty. Listen, I've been trying to place your accent. Where are you from?"

"Baltimore. See you in twenty minutes." Flashing her bright smile, she turned and walked across the hall.

He gazed after her. He had a hunch she hadn't been a housekeeper back in Baltimore. Everybody had a story, and he wanted to know hers.

KERI RETREATED TO her room so she could give herself a good talking to while she showered off the grime. She was attracted to Michael, and she needed to put a lid on that inconvenient attraction ASAP. She was a member of the staff, which meant no fraternizing with the guests.

Nobody had told her that in so many words, but she'd been on the other end of the social spectrum. Her parents would have fired any maid who'd shown interest in a houseguest. It just wasn't done.

The Chances hadn't turned this upstairs bedroom into housekeeper's quarters so that she could mingle with the guests. They'd put her here because it was the only space available that also could be plumbed for a small bathroom. If she happened to be across the hall from the extremely good-looking Michael Hartford, she didn't have to emphasize the fact. God knew what he'd thought when she'd mentioned how close she was to his room.

When she took him on a tour, she'd establish more distance between them. The whole mouse incident had thrown her off and made her forget her position here. She'd even pushed the issue of burying the little rodent when Jack had clearly thought that was nonsense, and she'd made her stand in front of Michael. She'd apologize to Jack about that.

After years of being at the top of the social pecking order, she sometimes forgot that she wasn't there now, at least not in Jackson Hole. Then again, the Chance family didn't stand on ceremony with their employees. Back home, the household help wouldn't dream of calling their employers by their first names. At the Last Chance, first names were all anybody used.

That made it easy for her to forget that she wasn't in charge around here. She figured the Chances understood why she slipped up sometimes, though. They all knew that anytime she chose, she could tap into her trust fund. She was proud to say she hadn't needed to.

Eighteen months ago, on New Year's Eve, she'd scandalized Baltimore society by engaging in an epic girl fight at a ritzy party. Selena had started it, and Keri had finished it. Pictures of the fight had shown up on Facebook, and somehow Keri had become the villain of the piece.

When she could no longer be effective in her job at a Baltimore PR firm because of the gossip, she'd decided that a change of scenery might be a good idea. Wyoming had seemed far enough away to accomplish that, and she'd loved the area when the family had come for ski vacations. She'd flown to Jackson, rented a car and searched for a job.

Lucky for her, the Last Chance had taken her on, and instinct had told her to grab the opportunity. Sure, she could have lived off her trust fund while she was in Jackson Hole, but she'd wanted to see if she could make it on her own. She'd been a trust-fund baby for too long, and she hadn't realized how that steady income had undermined her confidence.

Earning a living without depending on anything but her own grit and determination had boosted her morale quite a bit. She didn't miss her old life much. She'd only intended to be here a few months, until the gossip had died down, but the place had grown on her.

Theoretically she could go back to Baltimore anytime, because according to her parents, nobody mentioned the incident anymore. But Keri found herself looking for excuses to stay at the ranch. They'd needed her when the boys had arrived in June, and now they needed her to help with the wedding guests.

Come winter, her services wouldn't be so critical. She could give her notice then, which would allow them plenty of time to find a new housekeeper. She loved living on the ranch, but she didn't intend to be a cleaning lady for the rest of her working life. What she did want was still up for debate.

She showered in record time, and true to her word, she made it out of her room and back over to Michael's in twenty minutes. She'd even managed to blow-dry her hair. Getting dressed was easy these days. Jeans, a T-shirt, running shoes. She no longer spent much time on makeup, either.

Some fancier outfits hung in her closet, but she had no reason to wear them. Once in a while she longed for a reason to put on party clothes, but people didn't do that much at the ranch, or in the little town of Shoshone ten miles down the road. She'd accepted dates with some of the ranch hands, but jeans were fine for the Spirits and Spurs in Shoshone. Those dates hadn't resulted in any wild love affairs, either.

Maybe that explained her attraction to Michael. He hailed from her neck of the woods, and she felt that gave them something in common that she didn't have with everyone here. As she rapped on his door frame to announce her presence, she cautioned herself to be very careful. She might not want to keep this job forever, but she didn't want to be booted out for inappropriate behavior, either.

Michael closed a drawer and turned. He'd taken off his hat and it lay on the bed, brim side down. She'd have to tell him to flip it the other way, which preserved the shape better.

He glanced at the clock sitting on top of the dresser. "Twenty minutes, and you're showered and changed. I don't think I know any woman who could accomplish that."

"It's the simplicity of the existence here. Ranch life can be complicated sometimes, but getting dressed for it isn't."

"Maybe not if you've been here long enough." He gestured toward his shirt, jeans and boots. "This outfit took an enormous amount of effort."

"It did? Why?"

"I didn't want to look like I just stepped out of a Western wear store, so I had someone rough these things up a bit. Everything's been artificially distressed so it looks as if I've been out riding the trails and roping those doggies."

She pressed her lips together, not sure if she was supposed to find that funny or not.

"It's okay. You can laugh. It makes me laugh, too."

"Whoever worked on it did a good job. When you walked through the front door, I thought you were the real deal."

"I'm not, but maybe Jack will whip me into shape."

"I'm sure he will, but why are you…" She caught herself just in time. Her question was inappropriate coming from a staff member.

"Why am I doing this?"

She shook her head. "Forget I asked. It's none of my business."

"Well, it's complicated."

"Really, you don't have to explain."

"I know, but it's a legitimate question. All my life I've wanted to be a cowboy. I can't really be one because my life is in New York City. But this week, I'll at least find out if I have what it takes."

"I completely understand that." Yep, that feeling of connection was snapping into place. She'd come out here to get away from gossip, but she'd stayed because she wanted to see if she had what it took to live in a completely different environment.

She was testing herself, and apparently, so was he. She admired that impulse to seek a different path from the one you were born to. Talking about that with him would make for interesting conversation. Maybe someday, when they were both back in their normal environments…but that was getting way ahead of the game.

"I believe that you do understand. I'll take a wild guess that you might have some similar reasons for being in Wyoming."

"Good guess." But she wouldn't elaborate, because the more they exchanged confidences now, the stronger the link between them. And now was not the time for making a connection. "Let's go see the rest of the house."

3

KERI WAS AN excellent tour guide, and Michael was interested in the history of the massive two-story ranch house with its sturdy log construction. But he was even more interested in Keri and why she'd left Baltimore to come out here. Whatever the reason, she'd adapted with a can-do attitude that both attracted and inspired him.

She kept the focus on the ranch, though, and he couldn't figure out how to question her without being intrusive. He learned about the grandparents, Archie and Nelsie Chance, who'd homesteaded the place in the thirties. As a storyteller, he appreciated the tale of how they'd taken a run-down place and created a gem that was now worth millions to their heirs. Jack was the oldest grandson, followed by Nick, a veterinarian, and Gabe, who specialized in showing the registered Paints bred and trained at the Last Chance. Raising cattle had been abandoned for the horse business.

Keri proudly showed off the awards Gabe had won, all displayed in a case in the large living room, which was anchored by a great stone fireplace. The leather furniture and wagon-wheel chandelier were the sort of rustic touches Michael often included in his books. He was gratified to find out that in this, too, he'd gotten it right.

But whenever he tried to turn the conversation in the direction of Keri's background, she dodged away. Close to six o'clock, she took him into a large dining room at the end of the house's left wing. His bedroom would be directly above it.

She gestured to four round tables, each of which could seat eight people. "This is where everyone gathers for lunch," she said. "That includes the ranch hands and as many members of the Chance family as are available. It's a tradition to get together for the noon meal and exchange information about ranch business."

"Do you eat lunch here, then?"

"That depends on whether Mary Lou needs my help. When the boys were here, they also ate in the dining room, so Mary Lou needed me to serve and clear."

"But now?"

"I grabbed a quick lunch in the kitchen today because I had so much cleaning to do, but tomorrow I'll probably eat here. Mary Lou may join everyone, too, at least for a few days until the wedding guests arrive. Then it'll get busy again."

Michael felt ridiculously pleased that he'd see her at lunch tomorrow. Between now and then he planned to do some research on the internet. Social media could be a pain in the ass, but through it he might be able to get a bead on Keri Fitzpatrick.

A regal woman with silver hair walked out of the kitchen. She wore jeans and a Western blouse, nothing fancy, but she had an air of command about her.

"I thought I heard voices." She walked forward, hand extended. "You must be Michael Hartford, Bethany's friend."

"And you must be Sarah Chance." He clasped her hand and felt the firm grip of a woman who was as sure of her place in the world as Jack was of his. Bethany had told him that Sarah was the reigning queen of the neighborhood, and Michael began to see why.

"That's right." She smiled at him. "Looks like Keri's been showing you around. Thanks for doing that, Keri. I've been a little distracted today. Pete wants to fly in floral arrangements from Hawaii, and I want wildflowers. I do believe it's our first fight."

Michael spoke without thinking. "Wildflowers." Then he realized he didn't have a vote. "Forget that. It's not my place to—"

"Hey, I'll take all the support I can get." Sarah glanced at Keri. "What do you think?"

"I agree with Michael. This is Wyoming. You need wildflowers, not some exotic tropical arrangement. But I'll bet Pete wants to do something extravagant because he's so happy. It's sweet, really."

"It is sweet." Sarah's blue eyes grew soft. "So maybe I'll let him order a tropical bouquet for me to carry, and the altar can be decked with wildflowers. How's that?"

"Perfect," Keri said. "Great compromise. And now, if you'll excuse me, I'll go in and see if Mary Lou needs any help in the kitchen." Just like that, she was gone.

Sarah turned to him. "How about a drink before dinner?"

"Sounds good." Not as good as following Keri into the kitchen, but he had no excuse to do that. Guests probably weren't allowed to help out, and he'd be worthless at it, anyway.

"Let's go back into the living room." She led him down the hall past a rogue's gallery of family pictures. "Pete should be here soon. He had some errands in town. Jack and Josie are coming, too. They've left little Archie over at Gabe and Morgan's house." She paused. "Here I am rattling off names, and I have no idea if you know who I'm talking about. Did Bethany fill you in at all?"

"I know the names of your sons, and Jack mentioned Josie and little Archie on the drive in."

"Morgan is Gabe's wife, and they have two kids, a girl and a boy. Nick is married to Dominique, and they have one adopted boy. All three of my sons have built their own homes on ranch land, and I love having them so close."

"You have quite a legacy here, Sarah."

"Thanks to Archie and Nelsie." She gestured around the living room as they walked in. "I married into this, so I can't take any credit for it."

"That's not what Keri said. She told me that you're the lynchpin holding everything together."

"Did she? What a nice thing for her to say." Sarah moved over to the liquor cabinet. "I do like that woman. I wish she'd stay on, but I can't expect someone with her background to be a housekeeper much longer."

"She's leaving?" Michael felt a moment of panic. If she took off tomorrow or the next day, he'd never have a chance to learn more about her.

"Oh, not right away, but she will. I think she's waiting until after the wedding, which is considerate." She opened the hand-carved liquor cabinet. "What would you like?"

"Two fingers of Scotch, if you have it."

"We do." In moments she'd poured herself a glass of red wine and given Michael a squat tumbler containing ice and his requested Scotch. "Here's to friendship."

"To friendship, and to your generosity in letting me stay here the week before your wedding."

She touched her glass to his and took a sip. "I'm thrilled you're here. Jack needed something to do this week, so your arrival is perfect. If he didn't have you to distract him, he'd be underfoot. He pretends not to like the preparation stage, but he can't keep his nose out of things, either."

Good thing Michael hadn't been drinking when she'd said that or he might have choked on his Scotch. No wonder Sarah was considered the lynchpin of the family. She understood people better than some CEOs he'd met.

She gestured toward the leather chairs positioned in front of the fireplace. "Let's sit. It's too warm for a fire, but we tend to gather here and stare at the cold grate, anyway. Habit, I guess." She settled into one of the leather armchairs.

Michael took the one next to her. "Great chair."

"Thanks."

"And even without a fire, the stonework is worth looking at."

"My father-in-law was a talented man." She turned to Michael. "I'm curious. What prompted you to ask for riding and roping lessons?"

Michael decided to give her the same answer he'd

given Keri. It was the truth, so far as it went. "Like a lot of guys, I've always wanted to be a cowboy."

She studied him for a moment. "It's not as glamorous as it looks from the outside."

"I'm sure it's not, which is why I don't plan to actually be one. But learning some of the skills will be... interesting."

She smiled. "I notice you didn't say it would be fun."

"Yeah, well, I don't know if it will be or not, but I have to try."

"I think it will be fun for you. I hope so, because you're obviously interested in giving it a shot. But Jack's a taskmaster."

"I'm not surprised to hear that." Michael took another taste of his Scotch, which was excellent.

"I think we have some liniment upstairs, and probably Epsom salts, too. Have Keri find those for you."

"Okay." He decided that was as good an opening as any. "If I'm being too nosy, just say so, but why are you so sure Keri will leave? What is her background?"

"She didn't tell you?"

"No, just that she's from Baltimore."

Sarah hesitated. "I shouldn't have mentioned that I think she'll leave. I'll blame being distracted by the wedding for letting that comment slip out. But since I did mention it, I can understand why you'd be curious. So I'll just say that she comes from a very privileged background." She glanced at him. "Probably much like yours, in fact."

"Yet she's working as a housekeeper."

"Yes, and her reasons are hers to tell."

"I don't think she will tell me."

Sarah met his gaze. "That's up to her, then."

Michael had no choice but to drop the subject. He asked about her grandchildren, a topic she clearly loved, and Keri wasn't mentioned again. Later on, Sarah's fiancé arrived, followed by Jack and his wife, Josie.

During their meal in the smaller dining room adjacent to the larger one used for lunch, Michael thought he did a pretty decent job of focusing on his four dinner partners. Pete Beckett, Sarah's fiancé, was tall, lean and had a great sense of humor. Josie, an attractive blonde, dressed like a cowgirl and wore her long hair in a braid down her back. Jack obviously needed a strong woman to balance his tendency to take charge, and Josie seemed to fit the bill. Michael liked them all, but his thoughts stayed with Keri.

The ranch cook, a middle-aged woman named Mary Lou, served the meal. But Michael knew that Keri had helped prepare it, and he kept hoping she'd show up at some point. She didn't, but he could hear the faint sounds of feminine laughter coming from the kitchen, along with a man's voice.

Michael wondered who was in that kitchen with Mary Lou and Keri. For all he knew, Keri was involved with one of the ranch hands. It shouldn't matter to him. Unfortunately for his peace of mind, it did.

THE DINERS HAD LEFT, the dining table had been cleared and Keri sat with Mary Lou in the kitchen. They'd been joined by Watkins, a ranch hand who was also Mary Lou's husband as of the previous summer. All three of them were enjoying a leisurely moment over dessert and coffee.

"Mary Lou, nobody can make a chocolate cake like you can." Keri pushed back her chair. "I'm having a second piece."

"Believe I'll have a second piece of that cake, myself." Watkins rose from his chair.

"Hold on there, cowboy." Mary Lou caught his arm and pulled him back down. "Your jeans are getting a might snug."

Watkins sighed and resumed his seat. "That's a fact, but it ain't fair." He used a napkin to wipe cake crumbs off his handlebar mustache. "Keri eats and eats, and she doesn't gain a pound. I just look at a second piece of cake and I have to let out my belt another hole."

"That's because Keri is twenty-seven and you're fifty-four," Mary Lou said. "Your metabolism is slower."

"That may be, Lou-Lou, but the rest of me hasn't lost a step." He winked at Mary Lou. Although they'd only been married a year, he'd been after her for a long time before that, and his delight at finally getting her was obvious.

Mary Lou rolled her eyes. "There you go again, bragging on yourself." But she said it with a smile. Then she glanced at Keri. "I thought you were getting more cake?"

"I don't really need it."

"Don't give it up just because Watkins will stare at you mournfully while you eat it. Be strong. Claim your cake."

"I will stare at her mournfully, too," Watkins said. "That is the best damn cake in the world."

"Oh, for crying out loud!" Mary Lou picked up his plate and hers. "I'll cut you a tiny slice, you whiny baby.

You can eat it slow. And I'll have some more, while I'm at it. Give me your plate, Keri. Might as well cut them all at once."

Keri grinned and handed over her plate. "Thanks, Mary Lou. Make it this big." She held her thumb and forefinger about two inches apart.

Watkins shook his head. "I don't know where you put it all, girl."

"It's the grave digging," Mary Lou said as she uncovered the cake and started slicing. "Keeps a person slim and trim."

"I guess I'll never live that down, will I?" Keri didn't mind the teasing, though. Mary Lou only teased the people she liked.

"You not only buried him, you erected a monument." Mary Lou set a good-size piece of cake in front of Keri, a medium-size one for herself and a sliver in front of Watkins, who made a face.

Keri picked up her fork. "Jack asked me to make sure the dogs couldn't dig it up."

Watkins laughed. "They sure as hell won't after you piled about twenty-five rocks on it. You'd need a backhoe to get that varmint out of the ground, now."

"But at least we know where she buried the little bugger," Mary Lou said. "I won't get a nasty surprise next summer when I plant my petunias." She glanced over at the door that opened onto the large dining room and lowered her voice. "Don't look now, but the greenhorn's on his way."

Keri's pulse jumped. She'd been thinking about Michael as he'd sat eating his meal with the Chance family in the formal dining room. She wondered how he'd liked the mashed potatoes, which she'd beaten until there were absolutely zero lumps. She usually didn't take such care with the potatoes.

Despite Mary Lou's warning not to look, Keri turned in her chair and her gaze met Michael's. She knew before he spoke that he'd come searching for her. Her pulse ratcheted up another notch. He was one good-looking man.

Mary Lou stood. "If you're after another slice of cake, you've come to the right place. We're all having seconds."

Michael took in the scene and hesitated for a moment. He didn't seem to have come there for cake. Then he smiled. "I'd love another piece. Thanks for asking."

"Have a seat next to Keri. I'll get it for you." Mary Lou opened a cupboard and took down another dessert plate.

Michael's presence next to Keri created a dramatic change in temperature. He also took up space, and she moved her knee so she wouldn't brush against his. She became aware of his slow, measured breathing and the scent of his aftershave. Until this moment, she'd avoided being close enough to smell it.

"Coffee?" Mary Lou asked.

"Sure. That would be great."

"Cream and sugar?"

"Just black."

His voice stroked her nerve endings, putting them on alert. She felt tension coming from him, too. If she had to guess, she'd say he was as hyperaware of her as she was of him. This would be an interesting week.

"I'm Watkins, by the way." The barrel-chested cowboy reached across the table to shake Michael's hand. "Mary Lou's husband."

"I'm so sorry!" Keri was mortified. "I should have introduced you two. I forgot Michael doesn't know everyone."

"Don't worry about it." Michael glanced at her with a smile. "I barged in here uninvited. I hope I'm not intruding."

"'Course not." Mary Lou set a piece of cake in front of him, along with a fork and napkin. "My kitchen's open to anyone on the ranch. Sooner or later, everybody comes through here."

"After tonight's meal, I can see why," Michael said. "Dinner was great. The mashed potatoes were perfect."

"Keri made those." Mary Lou poured coffee into a ceramic mug and brought it to the table.

Michael turned toward Keri again. "Well, you did a terrific job on them."

"Thanks." Keri's cheeks warmed. Men had given her compliments before, but never about her cooking. Until she'd moved here, she'd only known how to operate a coffeepot and a microwave. "Mary Lou's a good teacher."

"Apparently I am," Mary Lou said with a laugh. "You knew squat about cooking when you came, and now you're not half bad at it." She reclaimed her seat at the table.

"Yep." Watkins beamed at Keri. "You caught on real quick. Today you graduated to the mouse-burying business. Next thing I know, you'll be shoveling out stalls."

"Bring it on." Keri felt Michael's attention on her, and she tried to squash the squiggles of excitement that attention produced. "I've cleaned up after eight adolescent boys. Nothing scares me."

"Wish I could say the same." Michael picked up his fork and started eating his cake. "But Jack Chance scares the bejeezus out of me."

Watkins chuckled. "He likes doing that with greenhorns. You'll be okay."

Michael swallowed a bite of cake and reached for his coffee. "That's what I told myself, until Sarah mentioned the liniment and Epsom salts. Now I'm worried." He turned toward Keri. "She said you'd find them for me. That's why I came looking for you. I'm glad I did."

Her breath caught at the unmistakable flicker of desire in his eyes. "Yeah, you got an extra piece of cake out of the deal." She hoped Mary Lou and Watkins hadn't noticed her tone was slightly strained.

"Exactly." His gaze held hers for one more heart-stopping moment. Then he broke eye contact and went back to eating his cake and asking questions about the ranch as if nothing of significance had passed between them.

But, oh, it had. She started to pick up her coffee mug and had to wait a moment until she stopped trembling. Good Lord. She wanted this man, and he wanted her right back. They'd be sleeping across the hall from each other for a week. Keeping a lid on this mutual attraction was going to be a real challenge.

4

AFTER A COZY half-hour spent eating cake and drinking coffee in Mary Lou's kitchen with Keri sitting right next to him, Michael's defenses were down. Circumstances had presented him with rich chocolate, a tempting woman and the prospect of going upstairs with her after they'd finished their dessert. A guy could only take so much before he cracked.

On top of that, he discovered that Mary Lou and Watkins had only been married a year, which explained the friskiness going on between them. Knowing that Mary Lou and Watkins would soon be getting it on didn't help Michael's state of mind. They shooed both Keri and Michael out of the kitchen once the dishes were cleared from the table.

That left them little choice but to walk through the silent house and climb the stairs together. The intimacy of it grew with each step they took. Michael made small talk along the way, and Keri responded as if she thought his conversation was brilliant.

She wasn't fooling him, and he doubted that he was fooling her, either. They were on thin ice, but maybe if they didn't acknowledge that, they'd get to their respective bedrooms without incident. What a damned inconvenient time to lust after a woman.

They kept up the inane chatter, but the winding staircase seemed endless. She was a step ahead of him, and her scent, a combination of sweet perfume and warm woman, drifted back to him, tugging at his resolve. He considered laying a hand on her shoulder. That might be all it would take.

She'd turn back to him, and then…then he would kiss her. But it wouldn't stop with a kiss, and he knew that. He'd never made love to a woman on a staircase, and he wasn't about to do it now. Still, that didn't keep the images from bombarding him until he was hard and aching.

"Do you want me to dig out the liniment and Epsom salts tonight, so you'll have them available when you come back from riding tomorrow?"

"Sure." He shouldn't have said that. Every extra minute they spent together increased the possibility that one of them might do something that would make them both lose control. He was willing to take that risk if he could be with her a little bit longer.

"I think they're in your bathroom." She walked down the hallway, lit only by a small wall sconce.

He followed, all the while lecturing himself to get a grip on his libido. This wasn't like him. Then again, she wasn't like any woman he'd met before. She had secrets, and he had to believe they were interesting secrets. Apparently curiosity was a powerful aphrodisiac for him. He hadn't known that.

Well, then, that was the solution, wasn't it? If he

solved the mystery of Keri Fitzpatrick, he wouldn't be so attracted to her. He'd planned on searching the internet to see what he could turn up, but asking her outright was really a more honest way to approach it. His questions might be considered intrusive, but if that would keep him from seducing his host's housekeeper, he felt justified.

She stepped into the bathroom and flipped on the wall switch. "Let's see what I can find." Walking over to the sink set into a carved wooden vanity, she began pulling open drawers.

He leaned in the doorway. "It's none of my business, but wondering why you left Baltimore to come out here and be a housekeeper is driving me crazy."

"It is?" She glanced up and understanding passed between them without either of them saying a word. His curiosity wasn't the only thing driving him crazy, and they both knew it. "The answer's pretty simple," she said. "I ran away from a scandal."

"That's not a simple answer." And all it did was ratchet his curiosity up a notch.

She gave him a wry smile. "No, I guess not." Folding her arms, she propped one hip against the vanity. "I was at a New Year's Eve party at a friend's penthouse and the champagne was flowing. This cute guy and I were making out in a darkened corner when his fiancée showed up. I didn't know he was engaged."

"That was the scandal?" He had a hard time imagining that would create enough gossip to make her leave town.

"No. She threw a drink in my face, so I threw one in hers. She came at me, claws out, wailing like a banshee.

My temper got the best of me, and…well, there was smashed crystal, imported caviar ground into the antique rug, a crack in a priceless statue…in other words, an unholy mess."

Michael tried not to grin, but she'd conjured up quite a picture. He'd only known her a short while, but he sensed the fire in her. She wouldn't take kindly to being falsely accused. "And here I was impressed that you didn't faint over a mouse."

She shrugged. "What can I say? I'm Irish."

He'd thought learning her secrets would make her less intriguing. Instead, he was more fascinated than ever. "Did you win?"

Triumph shone briefly in her green eyes. Then she sighed. "I did. But in the end, I lost, because I became notorious as the New Year's Eve Brawler. I couldn't do my job without the subject coming up. That fight began to define who I was."

"What's your profession?"

"PR."

It figured that she'd be trained in the area that was currently the scourge of his existence.

She pushed away from the vanity. "There you have it, the reason I came out here." Moving to the other side of the vanity, she opened the top drawer.

"But why be a housekeeper? Why not get another PR job?"

"I just wanted to hide out for a while, do something completely different. The cliché for it is *finding yourself.* I hadn't been all that happy with my life in Baltimore, anyway, so this was a chance to explore other options."

"You came out here without knowing a soul?"

"Yep. That was exciting, in a way. I interviewed for the job here on a whim. I had no experience, but luckily Sarah and Jack took pity on me." She rummaged in the drawer. "There's a box wedged in the back of this drawer. It could be the liniment."

"For the record, Sarah's thrilled with the job you're doing."

"She said that?" Keri reached deep into the drawer and tugged at the box. It was more square than rectangular, which didn't make sense for a tube of ointment, but she might as well haul it out, anyway.

"She did. She's very happy with your work, but she also expects you to leave."

"Which I will, but I'll give them plenty of time to hire someone else before the boys descend on them next summer." She yanked at the box. "Got it!" Holding it aloft, she looked at the label.

Michael looked, too, and began to laugh. "That's not liniment."

Without meeting his eyes, she tossed the box back in the drawer. "Nope, not liniment." Her cheeks had turned a becoming shade of rose.

Michael longed to walk over there and kiss her blushing cheeks, her full mouth and her delicate throat. Hell, he'd like to work his way through every tempting spot on her sweet body. Each piece of the puzzle that was Keri Fitzpatrick only made him want to find more so he could complete the picture.

"I'll keep looking." She opened the door under the sink and crouched down to peer inside.

"That's okay." God, he was a noble SOB. "I may not

even need any. We should probably just forget about it
and go to bed."

She gave him a startled glance. "What?"

Oh, Keri. Lust slammed into him. He pushed it back.
"Separately."

"Oh." She blushed again. "Right."

"See you in the morning." He walked out of the bathroom before he changed his mind and closed the short
gap between them. Yes, he was nobler than he ever
thought he could be.

But once he was inside his room with the door closed,
he reflected on what had been in that drawer. Fate had
not only thrown the luscious Keri into his path, it had
provided him with condoms.

KERI TURNED OFF the bathroom light and retreated to
her room. Once there, she flopped back on the bed and
stared up at the ceiling until her head stopped buzzing
and her heartbeat returned to normal. She'd given herself away. How embarrassing was that?

A woman who wasn't thinking about sex would
never have reacted the way she had when Michael had
suggested they go to bed. People said that kind of thing
all the time—*we should go to bed*—and they only meant
it was time to turn in. That's all Michael had been saying, for God's sake. She was the one who'd made it into
something else.

Sure, there was a sexual attraction between them. For
the benefit of all concerned, they would ignore that attraction. No good would come of indulging themselves.

Not true, a devilish voice taunted her. *Lots of good
would come. And you would, too, most likely.*

Her groan was spiced with laughter. She'd behaved like a nun ever since taking the job at the Last Chance. A woman living in her employer's house couldn't exactly invite guys up to her room. To be honest, she hadn't met anyone she'd wanted to invite in. Until now.

The whole setup was ridiculous. If she'd met Michael while on some business trip to New York and they'd hit it off this well, she would have considered a sexual relationship. Maybe not tonight, because that was a bit fast. Tomorrow night wouldn't have been out of the question.

But they weren't in New York. They were across the hall from each other in the Chance family's ranch house, where she was an employee and Michael was a guest. No matter which way she sliced it, that put him off-limits.

So she should be patient. He would leave at the end of the week, and she would leave in a couple of months. She'd get his contact information and give him hers. If the chemistry between them was more than a passing fancy they could get together later, once the barriers had been removed.

Since they were from similar backgrounds, and apparently had both yearned for a more unfettered lifestyle out West, they'd probably have many traits in common. She admired him for throwing himself into this setting with no experience. That took guts, and she appreciated a man with courage. Yes, he'd be worth tracking down later on.

Figuring out that a possible hookup was being postponed, not abandoned, should have made her feel less frustrated, but it didn't. Blowing out a breath, she levered herself off the bed and changed into her pajamas. Then she washed her face and brushed her teeth.

Unfortunately, she spent all that time straining to hear Michael moving around in his room. At one point she caught the sound of footsteps in the hall. Like a teenager with a crush, she pressed her ear to the door.

He went into the bathroom and closed the door. Calling herself crazy, she listened until he came out and started back down the hall. He paused, and she held her breath. What would she do if he knocked on her door?

She had two choices—to answer it, which might lead to the forbidden pleasures she dreamed of, or to ignore it, which was the wisest course of action and sounded dismal and sad. But he took the choice away from her by continuing into his room and closing the door. Damn.

With nothing exciting on the horizon, she climbed into bed and picked up the paperback by Jim Ford lying on her nightstand. One of the ranch hands she'd dated last fall had loaned her a Jim Ford Western to help teach her about ranch life.

She'd never read that kind of book before, and it had helped her feel more at home here. She'd liked the story, too. She'd ordered all of the Jim Ford books online, which had given her a stack of more than twenty.

Her nightly reading habit was her little secret, her stealth method of taking a crash course in all things Western. After going through them once, she'd started over, which probably qualified her as a fan.

She'd nearly finished this one, *Showdown at the Wildcat Saloon,* for the second time. Within twenty minutes she'd arrived at the last page. The good guys won, the bad guys lost and the cowboy hero ended up with the girl. The plot was more complicated than that, but the structure was similar in all the books.

That worked for Keri. She liked knowing the stories would turn out well, and the details about cowboys and ranch life had taught her many things she might not have learned otherwise. The hands at the Last Chance were too busy being cowboys to stop and explain the process to a transplant from Baltimore, but Jim Ford did a fine job.

Her only complaint was that the love scenes weren't hot enough to suit her. Maybe Western writers weren't expected to have spicy romance in their books, but she would have liked more sizzle. She'd considered writing to tell him so, but hadn't taken the time.

After finishing the current book, she glanced at the author photo on the inside back cover of the paperback. In it, Jim Ford leaned against the weathered side of a barn. She knew the photo well after seeing it in twenty-some books.

But tonight it reminded her of someone else. When she'd stared at the picture for a few minutes and couldn't place where she'd seen the guy, she turned out the light and slid down under the covers.

Lying there quietly, she could hear noises from Michael's room—the sound of his booted feet on the wooden floor, followed by the clump of the boots as he pulled them off and dropped them. She imagined him undressing, and then stopped imagining it. A sexual buzz right now wasn't going to help matters any.

Surely he was exhausted by now. He'd flown east-to-west, so his body clock was probably out of whack.

It was much later for him than for everyone else on the ranch.

But he wasn't going to bed. Instead, he turned on his laptop. That chime was unmistakable. If Jack had given him the ranch's Wi-Fi password, he could be checking his email. Or his portfolio.

Though she'd told him a lot about her life tonight, she was woefully ignorant of his, other than Jack mentioning that he was loaded. He could have inherited his money or earned it himself. She had no idea which.

Usually a person gave some indication if they had a job. They'd reference it somehow, but Michael had been curiously mum on the subject. So maybe he lived off his investments, or his parents' investments. She'd known plenty of people who did that.

She could choose that route herself, but she wouldn't. Now that she knew what hard work was, she'd discovered that she liked it. She enjoyed ending the day feeling pleasantly tired and satisfied with what she'd accomplished.

When she left this job, she'd continue to cook and clean for herself, at least most of the time. She didn't want to lose her newly acquired skills. The life she used to have, with minions handling every routine maintenance task, had lost its appeal.

Sleep began to pull her under, but in that hazy moment before she drifted off, she realized who Jim Ford reminded her of. Michael. The two men looked very much alike, except Michael was clean-shaven and Jim Ford had a mustache. Talk about a crazy coincidence. Michael Hartford knew nothing about being a cowboy, and Jim Ford was an expert on the subject.

Maybe she should loan Michael a few of her Jim Ford books. They might help him the way they'd helped her. Jack's lessons were all well and good, but Jim Ford provided the lingo. Michael also might get a kick out of knowing that if he grew a mustache, he could impersonate a well-known Western writer.

Tomorrow she'd leave a book in his room, along with a note to check out the author photo on the inside back cover. That should make him laugh.

5

By LATE MORNING on the following day, Michael was hating life, and he hadn't even made it out of the corral. If he'd had some image of galloping across a meadow on Day One, he could kiss that fantasy goodbye. He'd spent at least an hour, probably longer, learning to saddle and unsaddle his assigned horse, Destiny.

Destiny had stood patiently while Michael practiced over and over under Jack's supervision. Mastering the bridle application had taken another big chunk of time. Jack had insisted, and legitimately so, that a rider needed to know these basics before climbing aboard. Jack was also a perfectionist in this regard. No student of his would get away with sloppy habits. No, sir.

Michael couldn't very well bitch about Jack's exacting attitude, either. The guy was offering his house and his services for free, out of the goodness of his heart. If Michael had been paying him, the dynamics would have been different, but under this program Michael kept his mouth shut.

Lack of sleep hadn't helped his concentration any, either. He'd planned to work on his current manuscript for an hour or so the previous night because his deadline loomed. Usually, working helped him wind down, except the chapter he'd faced had included—of course— a love scene.

He'd thought about Keri while he wrote the blasted thing, so by the end of the writing session the scene had been hotter than he usually made them. And he'd been equally hot. At least he'd finished the chapter and could move on to some action sequences tonight.

That was assuming he could sit long enough to type. The first portion of the actual riding part hadn't been bad—getting the horse to walk and then putting on the brakes. But then had come the torturous gait called the trot.

Michael had circled the corral endlessly while Destiny jolted every bone in his body. How naively Michael had written trotting into his manuscripts over the years. His characters were constantly trotting their horses here, there and everywhere.

His characters were also experienced riders who had somehow learned how to sit in the saddle without bouncing like a teenager on a trampoline. Michael wondered how in hell they'd accomplished that feat. Jack kept telling him to sit back and just move with the horse. Yeah, right. He wondered if a construction worker just moved with his jackhammer.

At least he wouldn't have to worry about being tempted by the lovely housekeeper. After today, his privates would be out of commission. He might not be in shape to have sex for a month.

"Okay, slow him down," Jack called out from his perch on the corral fence. "Walk him around a couple of times and we'll call it quits for now and head in to lunch."

Lunchtime meant seeing Keri again. Despite feeling achy and chafed, he brightened at that prospect. As he walked Destiny through the gate Jack held open, he thought about Keri's expression last night when she'd reached into the vanity drawer and pulled out a box of condoms. She'd been flustered and cute as the dickens.

"That's what I like to see after a trotting session," Jack said. "A big ol' smile on your face. You'll be happy to know we'll work on that gait some more after lunch. You're better, but still not good enough."

Michael hadn't realized he'd been smiling, but Jack's comment sobered him up real quick. "How about trying some roping instead? You know, switch things up a little."

"Yeah, but you're so close on the trot!" Jack turned to fasten the gate. "Another hour or so and you'll have it down!"

Another hour or so and he'd be in traction. "Maybe so, but I'd rather spend some time roping. I have a scene coming up in the next chapter where the hero ropes the villain. I'll probably do a better job with it if I've thrown a rope myself."

"You're working on something now?" Jack walked beside him as they headed toward the barn.

"I am. That's why I brought my laptop, so I could write while I'm here."

"Well, that's just special. I hadn't thought about you actually writing while you stayed here. I might need to get a plaque for the door of that room after you leave."

"You're kidding, right?" Michael pulled the horse to a stop at the hitching post.

"No, not really. But I wouldn't do it because you want these lessons to be hush-hush. By the way, you can climb down from there anytime, now."

"Oh. Okay." Michael felt a little shaky and hoped to hell he didn't fall off.

"Left side, Hartford. Left side."

"Um, yeah. I was thinking about something else." He put his foot back in the left stirrup and eased his right foot free.

"Don't let yourself think about something else when you're working around horses, my friend. You're dealing with a thousand-pound animal. Anything can happen."

"Anything?" Michael thought Jack said things like that mostly to scare him. Clenching his jaw against the pain in his thigh muscles, he swung down from the saddle. He'd be damned if he'd let out a groan.

"Absolutely anything." Jack wore his dark glasses and his black Stetson, which made him look like a bad-ass. "Death, dismemberment, you name it."

"That really makes me want to get back on old Destiny."

"Ah, I'm just having a little fun. You're safer on him than you are walking down the streets of New York City. But I'll bet you stay alert there."

"I do."

"That's really all there is to it. Be vigilant when you're around horses. Don't be scared. Be aware. Destiny's calm, but no telling what kind of horse you'll end up with for the photo shoot. Some horses spook at a blowing scrap of paper."

"It's good advice. Thanks."

"You're welcome. Don't want you getting killed." He grinned. "Aside from my concern for you as a fellow human being, I'd miss out on more Jim Ford books."

"You're all heart, Jack."

"So they tell me." He gestured toward Destiny. "Take off his saddle, and we'll have a short lesson in grooming before we turn him loose in the pasture. We'll rope this afternoon if that's what floats your boat."

Thank God. "I appreciate that."

"I suppose you'll need to rope somebody, if that's what you'll be writing about."

"A post will do fine. I don't need to actually—"

"Oh, I think you do. For authenticity's sake."

Michael glanced at him. "Are you volunteering?"

"Hell, no. I'll volunteer one of the ranch hands. Tell me how big your villain is, and I'll find somebody that size."

"He's about your height."

"Hmm. Okay. Maybe Jeb, then."

"How are you planning to explain this little exercise without telling him I'm a writer?"

Jack gazed at him. "I see your point. We don't generally rope people around here. Jeb might very well question what we were up to." He sighed. "Guess I'll have to do it, after all."

"You don't have to. A post will work."

"No, it won't. There's a world of difference between roping a post and roping a man. I want you to get it right."

"Okay." Michael worked hard to keep from smiling. "If you insist." His day was looking up.

He followed Jack's instructions and brushed Destiny's glossy coat before turning him loose in the pasture. Destiny seemed as glad to be free of Michael as Michael was to be through with Destiny, at least for today. Michael looked at the experience from Destiny's perspective and realized that having a beginner rider bouncing on your backbone might not feel so good.

Following Jack's lead, Michael washed his hands and face in the deep sink located inside the barn. As they walked up to the ranch house, Michael felt almost like a cowboy. His clothes were dusty, he smelled of horse and he walked slightly bowlegged thanks to his riding lesson.

Like Jack, he kept his hat on as they mounted the steps, crossed the covered porch and went through the massive front door. On the way down the hall he pulled the brim a bit lower. Yeah. He was getting into this. He wondered if Keri would notice the difference.

KERI HAD A basket of hot rolls in each hand when Jack and Michael strode into the dining room. And they were definitely striding, not merely walking. Jack had always had that cocky way of moving, and now Michael had picked it up.

She was mesmerized by the sight of Michael, who obviously was in the process of getting his cowboy on. She'd promised herself to stop mooning over him, but how could she help it if he ramped up his sexy quotient when she wasn't looking? He even wore his hat with more authority. He'd spent the morning with a powerful horse between his legs, and she knew from her year at the ranch that riding could turn a regular guy into a conquering hero.

His gaze found hers and he smiled. Wow, did he ever look like Jim Ford when he did that. She'd left the book in his room, but he might not see it until this afternoon when he was finished working with Jack.

After returning his smile, she snapped out of her daze and delivered the rolls to two of the tables. Then she walked back into the kitchen. The ranch hands were hungry and she couldn't dawdle. Platters of fried chicken and bowls of potato salad and coleslaw sat on the counter. Mary Lou opened the large commercial oven and took out the first of the apple pies.

She set it on the only vacant space left on the counter and glanced at Keri. "Are you okay? You seem a little distracted."

"I'm fine. Sorry for the delay." She picked up two platters of chicken and hurried out the door. Mary Lou had come to depend on her to serve lunch, and unless she moved the main course out, no counter space was available for dessert.

Sarah used to help, but she'd done less as Keri took over her duties. This week Sarah was so involved with wedding plans that she wouldn't have been much use, anyway. Both the ceremony and the reception would take place at the ranch, and the details surrounding that production were endless.

Once Keri was back in the dining room, she couldn't help noticing where Michael had ended up. He and Jack had chosen the table where the ranch foreman, Emmett Sterling, sat with his daughter, Emily—who would be foreman someday—and her husband Clay Whitaker, who ran the stud program for the Last Chance. Four ranch hands rounded out the eight-place table.

Michael fit right in. The clothes he'd paid to have distressed were a little dirty from being out in the corral, which gave them more legitimacy. He joked with the people at the table as if he'd been part of this world forever. Not every city boy could pull that off, but Michael seemed to be a natural at it. Maybe he didn't need to read the Jim Ford books, after all.

She approached his table with a platter of chicken and a bowl of potato salad. The ranch hands ate family style and passed the serving dishes around. In fact, lunch at the Last Chance had always seemed like a big family gathering to Keri, and she loved the idea that everyone was on equal footing here.

She wasn't treated as a waitress, which meant she could pause beside Michael's chair and ask him how the morning went.

"Great." He gave her another one of those smiles that made him look like Jim Ford without the mustache. "Jack's teaching me a lot."

"Good. By the way, I left a book in your room, something that you might enjoy. I put it on your nightstand."

"Thanks. What is it?"

"A Western by Jim Ford. It's the perfect thing to read while you're here."

Michael must have swallowed wrong at that moment, because he launched into a coughing fit. One of the ranch hands got up and pounded him on the back while Jack offered him a glass of water. Keri stood and waited for the fit to be over, because she couldn't simply walk away as if she didn't care that he was choking. He wasn't turning blue, so she wasn't terribly worried, but it was a spectacular fit, all the same.

At last he settled down, took off his hat and wiped his eyes. "Sorry about that." He looked up at her. "Thanks for loaning me the book."

"I'm sure you'll like it."

"I'm sure I will."

"Well, I need to get back to the kitchen." She turned to go, but not before she caught a look passing between Michael and Jack. She didn't have time to interpret it because not everyone had food, and hungry cowboys looked forward to this meal. For many of them it was the highlight of their day.

Much later, after the pie had been devoured with many words of praise for Mary Lou's cooking, the ranch hands began filing out of the dining room. Keri was clearing the dishes when Jack approached. Michael wasn't with him.

"I didn't know you were a Jim Ford fan," he said.

"I am. Jeb loaned me one of his books and I've been hooked ever since." She decided this was the perfect time to talk about the mouse incident. "About that mouse. I probably shouldn't have made a stand in front of a guest. I apologize."

Jack waved a hand dismissively. "You were right to give those boys the benefit of the doubt. I'm too cynical sometimes."

"You could be right, too. It might have been an elaborate joke."

"It doesn't matter. The mouse has been decently interred." Jack shoved his hat back with his thumb. "How long have you been reading Jim Ford?"

"Since last October. I ordered every book that was available. They helped me understand ranch culture and I thought maybe they'd help Michael, too." She paused. "You know what's amazing? Michael actually looks like the picture of Jim Ford in the back of his books, except for the mustache. Is that wild or what?"

Jack opened his mouth as if to say something, but he closed it again. "Yes," he said at last. "I noticed that, too. Weird, huh?"

"Yes, totally weird." But she'd seen something in Jack's eyes that made her start to wonder. Michael couldn't possibly be Jim Ford. Considering Jim Ford's expertise, that made no sense.

Yet something was up. She could sense it. Jack and Michael had exchanged that significant glance at the table, as if they shared some kind of secret. She began weaving all kinds of scenarios. What if the real Jim Ford was an ugly old man who didn't photograph well? What if he'd asked Michael to masquerade as Jim Ford, and now Michael had to learn some ranch skills to make the charade believable?

She decided to keep her eyes and ears open. If that meant keeping tabs on Michael Hartford, so be it. That wouldn't be a hardship at all.

6

Roping looked so easy in the movies that Michael had expected to pick it up really fast. He played a mean game of racquetball, so he considered himself as co-ordinated as the next guy. But he soon discovered that *building a loop,* as Jack phrased it, was much harder than it looked. And he had to build a loop before he could throw it at anything.

"You're making it too big," Jack said. "Start smaller."

"A small loop looks wimpy."

"A big loop that's snarled around your ankles looks a hell of a lot worse. You wouldn't want anybody to think you're compensating for something with that big loop, would you?"

"Hey!"

"Just sayin'. Make one about half that size and see how you do."

Michael found the smaller loop worked much better. He made the rope spin in a circle next to him for a couple of seconds before it went all wonky again.

"Nice job. Keep playing around with that size while

I check on Bandit. He pulled a tendon and I want to see if the swelling's down any."

Michael kept his eye on the twirling rope. "Bandit's your horse?"

"My stallion."

"Oh, ho!" Michael was proud of himself for keeping the rope turning in a perfect circle as he talked. "A *stallion,* you say? Now who's compensating, Jack?"

"Nice comeback! Now you're starting to sound like a cowboy." Chuckling to himself, he started toward the barn.

Smug bastard. He'd earned the right to be, though. Michael envied his confidence and skill. He decided to throw all he had at this practice session so he'd have something to show for it when Jack came out of the barn.

Jack had said Michael would start by roping a nearby post. Then he'd progress to roping Jack. Michael gathered the rope, built his loop a little bigger and tossed it at the post.

He missed, but he'd expected that. He missed five times in a row, but on the sixth try, he roped the post. Okay, then. After he'd roped it three out of five attempts, he increased the size of his loop. He was getting the hang of it, now.

The rope spun in a circle wide enough so that it would fall neatly over Jack, hat and all, when he reappeared. Twirling the loop, Michael moved a little closer to the barn. He heard Jack's boots on the barn's wooden floor. Any second now he'd step into the sunshine, and then Michael would nail him.

His timing had to be perfect. Jack appeared. Michael let fly with the rope. It sailed toward Jack's head, knocked off his hat and dropped toward his shoulders.

"Pull on it!" Jack yelled.

Michael yanked the rope. It tightened quickly, but by then it was around Jack's knees.

"Shi-i-i-t!" Jack went down hard.

"Damn!" Dropping the rope, Michael ran forward. "Sorry! Are you okay?"

Jack pushed himself onto his knees, shook his head once to clear it and grinned up at Michael. "Congratulations, greenhorn." He leaned over and loosened the rope around his knees. "You just roped yourself a man."

"Yeah, but I knocked you down." Michael extended his hand to help him up. "I didn't mean to do that."

"Effective, though." Jack allowed Michael to pull him up. Then he dusted off the seat of his jeans. "Can't say I've ever had that particular experience. Can't say I'd want to do it again, either. But you'd want your hero to do that on purpose."

"Guess so."

"Sure you would. The hero takes the villain by surprise, waits until the rope drops to the guy's knees and then bam!" Jack smacked his fist into his palm. "The bad guy goes down, your hero runs over, gives him a right hook to the jaw and your villain's subdued."

Michael nodded. "That works. Thanks, Jack."

"You're welcome. Now I've made my contribution to art for the day."

Michael coiled the rope. "How's Bandit?"

"Doing okay. Come on in the barn and I'll introduce you."

Following Jack, Michael realized that even though

this was his first full day, he was starting to feel at home around here. The scent of hay mingled with the earthy smell of horses was familiar to him now. Sure, his muscles were sore and would probably tighten up on him later. But he'd taken his first two lessons in cowboying and hadn't done half bad.

"This is Bandit." Jack tucked his dark glasses into his shirt pocket, opened the stall door and walked up beside a big horse with distinct black-and-white markings, including a black circle around each eye. His right front leg was wrapped in a bandage. "Bandit, this is Michael, the tenderfoot I was telling you about."

"I'm happy to meet you, Bandit."

"Come on in," Jack said. "He likes to be scratched on his neck, like this." He demonstrated and stood back.

Michael mimicked Jack and scratched Bandit's silky neck. Maybe it was his imagination, but the horse seemed to exude power and confidence, much the way Jack did. "I take it you breed him."

"Yeah, we do." Jack stroked Bandit's nose. "He commands a high stud fee, which helps keep us in the black. So he gets the royal treatment around here."

"I'll bet he would, anyway."

Jack smiled in acknowledgment. "He would. We all have our favorites around here, and Bandit's mine. We've had some great times together over the years."

A moment ago Michael had been feeling a part of this environment, but that last statement told him how much of an outsider he was. He'd lived in apartments all his life, where the only animals he'd known well had been small dogs that walked down crowded sidewalks on leashes.

Jack had spent many solitary hours riding this majestic horse over the untamed acreage of the Last Chance Ranch. Michael had written about such rides, but that wasn't remotely the same as doing it. Now that he'd had a small taste of ranch life, he wanted to vault over the beginner stage he was currently in and take those long rides in the shadow of the Grand Tetons.

"We should probably talk about Keri," Jack said.

"What about her?" Michael glanced around to see if anyone else was in the barn.

"Don't worry. I checked. We have some privacy. That was the main reason for getting you in here." Jack continued to stroke Bandit's nose. "Keri's read everything you've written. Furthermore, she thinks you're the spitting image of Jim Ford, except for the mustache."

Michael blew out a breath. "Damn. She's going to figure this out. She's too smart not to." He debated his choices. "Can she keep a secret?"

"I would say so. I haven't noticed any blabbermouth tendencies."

"And she knows what it feels like to be embarrassed by negative publicity."

Jack glanced over at him. "She told you about the girl fight?"

"Yeah."

"Man, I would've loved to see that. She keeps a lid on her temper most of the time around here, but I found out the hard way she's murder in a snowball fight."

"I'll bet." Michael could picture her, cheeks pink from the cold, pelting the enemy with deadly accuracy.

"Anyway, she must like you. She doesn't broadcast

that information much. Other than you, she's only told me and Sarah, so far as I know."

"Well, I did ask her why she'd left Baltimore."

"She could have dodged the question or made up some bogus answer." Jack combed Bandit's forelock with his fingers.

"I think she feels a kinship to me because we're both from back east," Michael said. "And she knows I have a similar background. I can put myself in her shoes and imagine what she's been through."

Jack chuckled. "That could be true, but she also plain likes you. I haven't seen her look at any of the hands the way she looks at you."

Hearing that gave him a jolt of pleasure, but he didn't want Jack getting the wrong impression. "Just so you know, she hasn't said or done anything inappropriate."

"That sounded kind of protective." Jack's grin flashed. "I think maybe you like her, too."

"Yeah, I like her, but that's as far as it will go. I give you my word on that, Jack."

"Oh, for Pete's sake. This is the Last Chance, not the Waldorf Astoria. You told me on the drive from the airport that you can't seem to hook up with anyone you like."

"Yes, but hooking up with someone is not why I'm here."

"Hell, I know that! But if the opportunity presents itself, don't be such a damned puritan, okay? Near as I can tell, poor Keri hasn't been getting any since she arrived. Seems to me you could do each other a lot of good."

"I can't believe you're saying this."

"Apparently I have to. Otherwise you and Keri will spend a miserable week sleeping right across the hall from each other and doing nothing about it."

"Probably because she respects you and doesn't want to get fired! And I don't want to abuse your hospitality! Those are legitimate reasons. And I'm not a damned puritan."

"Okay, okay. I appreciate your code of honor, but I'm giving you permission to bend it. I'm giving her permission, too, but I can't very well talk to her, seeing as how I'm her boss and it would embarrass both of us. So I'm talking to you, sunshine. You can pass the word on to her."

Michael stared at him. "Pass the word on?"

"Well, use some finesse. You're the guy with the gigantic vocabulary, so I'm sure you can manage. But you'll have to tell her I said it was fine so she won't be afraid I'll fire her."

"That'll be an interesting discussion." Michael was having a tough time imagining it. He couldn't think of any subtle way to broach the subject.

"You'll figure it out. And if she's willing, and you'll have to be the judge of that, then cut loose a little while you're here. Trust me, it'll be good for you."

Michael nearly choked. "Are you telling me I need to get laid?"

"You said it. I didn't. But from the way you were whining about your situation yesterday afternoon, I'd have to answer in the affirmative. I didn't think this trip could help you any in that department, but then I noticed Keri had that certain look in her eye, and I recalculated your chances."

Michael scrubbed a hand over his face. "God."

"I'm not, despite rumors to the contrary. Oh, and FYI, there's a box of condoms somewhere in that bathroom."

Michael decided against mentioning that he already knew about those. "Any more tips?"

He was being sarcastic, but Jack didn't seem to notice. "Not at the moment, but if she's been reading all those Jim Ford books, she probably has a cowboy fantasy going on. You might want to play to that."

"I don't see how I can. Once she finds out Jim Ford's a phony, she's liable to be disappointed in both the books and in me."

"Look, she knows you're a tenderfoot, and she likes you, anyway. I'm guessing when she finds out the truth, she'll take pity on you."

Michael groaned. "Oh, that sounds even better."

"It could be. She's spent a year around cowboys. Ask her for pointers. Take it from ol' Jack—women love giving pointers to a man. Then the more you act like a cowboy, the more she'll feel proud of you and turned on at the same time. You're in an ideal position, my friend."

"I don't know if I agree with that. I think I could get squashed like a bug."

"Why should you? You have talent. You just managed to rope me without half trying."

"Oh, I was trying, Jack."

"See what you can do when you put your mind to it? You're more of a cowboy than you think you are. Just follow your instincts. And for God's sake, have fun. You take things way too seriously."

"I do?"

"Yeah, and I know all about the dangers of taking life too seriously. You miss all the good stuff. Don't do that."

THE DINNER HOUR came and went without Keri having any excuse to interact with Michael. She'd set the Epsom salts and the liniment on his bathroom counter, so he had no reason to ask for her help. She had cleaned up all the dinner dishes with Mary Lou and Watkins, both from their meal in the kitchen and the one served in the dining room.

With nothing left to do, she walked back through the house and climbed the stairs to the second floor. Michael's bedroom door was open and she could hear him moving around in there. But she couldn't think of any conversation she might need to have with him, so she opened her door and was halfway in when he called to her.

"Keri?"

The sound of his voice jump-started a familiar response of tingling heat that flowed despite her efforts to stem it. She had a thing for this guy, and apparently her hormones would dance to his tune whenever they had a chance. She turned. "Do you need something, Michael?"

"Yes." He stood in the doorway of his room, and his eyes, the gray-blue color of a jay's wing, focused intently on her. "I...need to tell you something."

"Is there a problem with your room?" She didn't think so, but it was her job to ask.

"No, it's about Jim Ford. Would you come in for a minute?"

A minute. He didn't have a lengthy discussion in

mind. But her pulse rate jumped at the thought of crossing his threshold. "Sure." She noticed that he hadn't said *Jim Ford's book.* He hadn't had time to read it, anyway.

No, he'd said *Jim Ford.* Her suspicion grew that for some reason he'd been asked to play the part of Jim Ford in public appearances. Maybe he was a wealthy actor she'd never heard of, although living close to New York most of her life, she knew the names of most of the famous actors on Broadway.

Once she walked into his room, he motioned her to the only chair, a wingback upholstered in a sturdy green plaid. He sat across from her on the edge of the bed. When he moved, a slight wince and crinkling of the corners of his eyes betrayed him. He needed that soak in the tub and some liniment before he went to bed.

But he'd given this "minute" with her priority, and she couldn't imagine why. Being here with him was exciting, though—the most excitement she'd had all day. His clothes looked much more lived-in than they had yesterday. Jack had put him through his paces.

No matter what he wanted to talk about, she was happy to sit and look at him. He had great shoulders, the kind a woman could take comfort from. His body was lean, but solid, too. She'd been surrounded by lean, solid male bodies for a year, but Michael's drew her more strongly than any of the others'.

Part of it was the combination of his clothes, which branded him a cowboy, and his accent, which reminded her of home. He was an enticing blend, which made him more exotic than any man she knew. But that wasn't all of it. Beneath his calm exterior, she sensed an undercurrent of primitive passion.

She'd sensed that undercurrent the minute he'd walked through the ranch house door. But until now, she hadn't admitted it or examined why she was so drawn to him. For years she'd battled that same untamed yearning.

Because of her polished society upbringing, she'd resisted those feelings and had blamed her Irish heritage for saddling her with inappropriate urges. Michael wasn't Irish, at least not that she knew, but that same hidden fire flashed in his eyes. It was there, now.

"So." He rested his hands on his jeans-clad knees, and tension radiated from him. "About Jim Ford."

"If I've caused a problem by bringing you his book, I apologize. I don't know why you're here, and I may have stumbled on something I shouldn't have. You can give me back the book, and we'll never talk about it again."

His glance flicked over her, and his mouth curved into a wry smile. "I don't think that's going to work. You're too intelligent, and I'll never be able to maintain my cover."

"You've been hired to impersonate him! I knew it!"

Humor glinted in his eyes. "That's one way of looking at it, but—"

"I won't give you away, Michael. I understand what it's like to have things you want to keep under wraps. You can trust me."

"I'm counting on it, because I'd rather not have anyone know I'm out in Wyoming learning how to be a cowboy."

"Of course. And I'll help you in any way I can. Have you read all of Jim Ford's books? Because I have, and I can fill you in on anything you might not know."

"I haven't read them."

"Then you'll really need my help, because I—"

"I wrote them. I'm Jim Ford."

Her mouth dropped open. Then she said the first thing that entered her mind. "No, you're not."

7

KERI WAS SO cute in her refusal to believe him that he almost laughed, but she wouldn't have appreciated that, so he controlled himself. "Yes, I'm afraid I am. I have the manuscripts on my laptop to prove it. My full name is Michael James Hartford, and I pulled the pseudonym Jim Ford out of that."

She still appeared to struggle with the information. "But Jim Ford is a cowboy. He's an expert. I've used his books to learn about ranch life, and everything he writes rings true to what I've found here. You—pardon me for saying so, Michael—but you're clueless!"

"That's a pretty accurate assessment." He tried not to get distracted by how beautiful she looked sitting there in the wingback. She'd worn a kelly-green blouse with her jeans today, and it matched her eyes. Her hair was in a ponytail, as it had been yesterday, but that only added to her appeal because it showed that she was no hothouse flower. She was a woman who was ready to take action, whether that meant defending herself in a girl fight, striking out on her own in Wyoming or hurling snowballs for fun. She would be an uninhibited lover, and he ached to experience that.

If Jack was right and Keri wanted him, she'd be the first woman he'd taken to bed who knew the real Michael Hartford. Every affair he'd had since he'd begun publishing the Jim Ford books had been based on a lie.

But at the moment, she didn't seem particularly interested in getting it on with Michael Hartford, aka Jim Ford. She looked confused and bewildered, like a kid who'd been told there's no Santa Claus.

She cleared her throat. "So all the while you've been writing the Jim Ford books, you've been making it up."

He couldn't keep from smiling. "That's what fiction writers do."

"Oh, for heaven's sake! I know that much! But what about your bio? It says you're a cowboy."

"No, it doesn't, not if you read it carefully. It says that I love the West and all it stands for—hard work, rugged living, honesty and straightforward dealings. It doesn't say I'm a cowboy or even that I live on a ranch."

"Then you're misleading people."

"I suppose you could say that, but they wouldn't buy the fantasy if I told them the truth about my life." This conversation wasn't going well.

"But you must have at least ridden a horse before."

"Nope. Not until Jack put me up on Destiny today."

"So it goes without saying that you've never roped a steer, shot a rifle or slept in a bunkhouse."

"Nope."

"How could you write like that, as if you'd done those things millions of times?" Her tone was more accusatory than curious. A spark of that Irish temper flared in her eyes.

"Lots and lots of research."

She continued to gaze at him as if he'd recently landed in a spaceship from a faraway galaxy. She didn't look as if she trusted him much, either. "So all this time, as I've been reading your books and picturing you as this accomplished cowboy, you've been...what?"

"Living on Central Park West."

"Do your books make that much money?"

"God, no. It's picking up, but that's not what pays the bills. I have a trust fund. The Hartfords are old money, and they wish to hell I'd stop writing trashy Westerns and go back to serving on the boards of prominent investment firms. It's what the Hartfords do."

She nodded. "I know that story. But I still don't understand why you didn't take some of that mega-money, buy a ranch and live the way your characters do. You obviously love the idea of it." She sounded impatient with him.

So here was the sticky part, where he could lay himself bare and risk being rejected as a coward, or make up some other story to explain his behavior. He was a pro at making up stories.

But he also was tired of lying to cover his ass. "I was afraid I wouldn't be any good at it."

"Really? But you already knew so much about this life."

"Book learning, as they used to say in the Old West. It's not the same."

"No, but you're a smart guy. You'd catch on. I was a

horrible housekeeper for the first couple of months, but people cut you some slack if you're trying."

He took a deep breath. "It's more than that. Sure I was afraid of making a fool of myself, especially after Jim Ford developed this reputation as a seasoned cowboy. But what if it turns out that I love the fantasy and not the reality? What if I don't like ranch life?"

Her eyes widened. "Oh. I didn't think of that. If the real thing ruined your fantasy, you wouldn't be able to write about it so lovingly, would you?"

"No."

"So why risk that now?"

"Couldn't avoid it." He told her about the PR campaign and his connection to Bethany. "She said I could trust Sarah and Jack to keep my identity secret while I learned enough to make it through the video."

"You can. You can trust me, too."

"I know."

"How do you know? We just met yesterday."

"Jack vouched for you."

"He did? That makes me feel good." She smiled, but then her smile faded. "Wait, if Jack vouched for me, then you two must have discussed whether to tell me your secret. Now I get why Jack was quizzing me about my Jim Ford books after lunch today. He was afraid I'd catch on."

"That's right. We decided I should tell you rather than you stumbling on to something when you were cleaning my room and finding out that way."

"I appreciate that."

This was his golden opportunity to segue into the

other topic, the more loaded one. His heart rate picked up. "That wasn't all that Jack had to say this afternoon."

Her cheeks turned pink. "If he mentioned that I overstep sometimes, he would be right. I've learned how to cook and clean, but sometimes I forget that I'm the hired help, not the mistress of the house. Old habits die hard."

"I'll bet, but that wasn't what we talked about. He… got the impression that you were…attracted to me." God, this felt like junior high. *He said you liked me. Do you like me?*

Her blush deepened and she looked away. "Okay, now I'm totally embarrassed. I'll talk to him tomorrow and assure him that I'm not making a play for his important guest. In fact, I should go back to my room right now." She stood quickly and started toward the door.

Michael left the bed. "He doesn't care."

She turned back to him, her face suffused with pink. *"What?"*

"He mentioned it because he thinks that would be fine. More than fine. He—"

"He *wants* me to make a move on you? That sounds bad on so many levels!"

"No! He didn't say that! This is coming out all wrong."

She folded her arms, and now she made no attempt to hide her temper. "No shit, Sherlock. Maybe you'd better tell me Jack's exact words instead of paraphrasing."

He thought about some of Jack's comments and winced. "I'm not sure that's a good idea."

"You can hardly make things worse."

"You have a point, there." He blew out a breath. "He

said that near as he could tell, you haven't been getting any since you came to work here."

Her green eyes glittered with fury. "That is none of his damned business, and first thing tomorrow, I'll tell him exactly that. I don't care if he fires me. I'll—"

"Keri, he meant it kindly. He noticed the chemistry between you and me and figured we'd both resist out of respect for him."

"Well, *duh*. I may forget my position sometimes, but I would never in a million years…" She peered at him. "Maybe you'd better tell me what you said to Jack on this topic."

"I told him I couldn't imagine how I'd ever broach the subject to you, and he claimed I have such a big vocabulary that I shouldn't have any trouble. Obviously he was wrong."

She kept her arms folded protectively over her chest, but her gaze grew speculative. "So basically, after Jack gave us the green light, you were ready to go along with his suggestion, assuming I agreed."

He tried to think of a way to reply that wouldn't land him in more hot water. But in the end, he decided that his new vow of complete honesty dictated that he could only give one answer.

"Yes." He looked into her eyes and hoped she'd see the desperate longing he felt every time she was near. "I've been lusting after you ever since you marched out of the house with that dead mouse."

Her mouth twitched as if she wanted to laugh but wouldn't let herself. "Smelly rodents turn you on, huh?"

"No, but a woman who's willing to dispose of them without freaking out certainly does. And if she's doing it out of a sentimental attachment to some adolescent boys, that's even more appealing. I figure a woman like that has character, and character turns me on."

Her rigid posture relaxed a little, although she didn't uncross her arms. The real change registered in her eyes. Hot indignation had been replaced by a different kind of heat. It flared for a moment, but she quickly looked away, as if she didn't want him to see. But he had, and that hot glance gave him hope.

"You've given me a lot to think about," she said.

"I'll bet."

"I left the Epsom salts and the liniment on the bathroom counter for you."

"I noticed. Thanks." He could be wrong, but that sounded as if she was about to make her getaway.

"Have a good night." She turned and walked out the door.

"Keri, wait." He followed her.

She turned, but kept her hand on the door into her room.

"If your answer is no, that's understandable. I'll only be here a week. You might consider that a bad deal all the way around."

She had the brass to look him up and down, as if considering her options. "Thanks for giving me a graceful way out. Even a woman who hasn't been getting any for the past year likes to give herself time to think things over."

"Keri, Jack didn't mean anything by that remark. He's a guy, and that's the way we talk."

"Uh-huh."

"I thought of something else, too. I'll only be here

for a week, but after you quit this job and move back to Baltimore, then—"

"Don't you think that's getting way ahead of ourselves?"

"Yeah." He rubbed the back of his neck. "Forget I mentioned it."

She didn't look as if she'd forget anything, especially not the lame parts of this conversation, which had been most of it. "For the record, have *you* been getting any lately, Michael?"

He felt warmth climbing up from his collar. "I'm kind of in your same boat."

"Hmm." She smiled. "That could make for an interesting combination. Good night." She opened her door, walked inside and closed it with a soft click.

He'd maintained control until her *interesting combination* remark. That got to him. He turned back to his room, his cock growing harder by the second. She was going to make him sweat out her decision, which meant he was in for another frustrating night.

But she hadn't said no. And the gleam in her eyes before she'd closed her bedroom door had definitely hinted at yes.

KERI CLOSED THE door and leaned her forehead against it as thoughts swirled in her mind. An hour ago, she'd had a crush on a hot guy who'd come to the Last Chance for a crash course in cowboy skills. Sure, she'd been frustrated that she couldn't pursue him because of her job, but there'd been some comfort in that, too. She could fantasize without repercussions.

Jack was absolutely right. She hadn't been getting

any for the past year, and she'd become used to being guy-less. Being without a man had given her time to think about where her life was going, and where she wanted it to go.

Until tonight, she'd figured on returning to Baltimore sometime this fall. But when Michael referred to it as a done deal, she was reminded of what waited for her there—more of the same. She could probably get her old job back and fall into the routine she'd left. She'd be a city girl again, wearing high heels to work and attending cocktail parties in sparkly dresses.

She remembered the constant hum of downtown Baltimore, the wail of a siren, the rattle of a jackhammer, the blare of a taxi, the rumble of a delivery truck. Walking over to her window, she raised it and listened. A cool pine-scented breeze billowed the curtains.

In the distance, an owl hooted. Some little night creature rustled in the bushes. Those sounds soothed her, whereas the mechanical noises in the city put her on edge. She'd never admitted that to herself before. When she ventured down to the harbor she felt closer to nature, but at the Last Chance she was immersed in it 24/7.

She edged closer to a decision that would change everything. She thought of her parents, but even when she'd lived in Baltimore she hadn't seen them all that often. She had friends in the city, too, but amazingly, she was more in sync with the people she'd met here. The life she'd once led seemed distant and unfamiliar. This place was her reality now, not the world she'd known back east.

Michael might be leaving in a week, but as she stood at the window gazing into darkness more complete than she'd ever find in the electricity-filled city, she knew what was right for her. She'd have to return to Baltimore to settle a few things, but after that, she was coming back to Wyoming.

That left her with another decision—what to do about the man across the hall. He'd thought she might guess his identity, but he was giving her too much credit. She'd been so firmly convinced that Jim Ford knew his stuff that she might never have figured out who Michael was.

Going over to her bedside table, she picked up the paperback she'd finished the night before and opened it to the author picture in the back. If she squinted so the mustache was blurry, she could clearly see that the man was Michael. Same broad shoulders, narrow hips, square jaw and sensuous mouth.

And he wanted her. As she studied his picture, sexual tension coiled low in her belly. He didn't just *want* her. He'd admitted to *lusting* after her. She believed him. He'd had that untamed look in his eyes when he'd said it. Her body had reacted to that look—it still hummed with anticipation.

Now that she knew who he was, she understood why he might have a wild side. After all, his characters did. She knew those guys, which gave her some insight into Michael. His characters were men of action, which she found very sexy. That's why she'd wanted more detail in the love scenes. That energy carried through a more explicit scene would be incredibly arousing.

Thinking about how he could improve those scenes aroused her even more. She was making herself squirm a little, to tell the truth. Relief was right across the hall. All she had to do was walk over there, and—her imaginary sexual adventure screeched to a stop when his door creaked open.

Was he coming back to mount another offensive? Her heart hammered as she waited to see what happened next. Footsteps padded down the hall. That was logical. He'd have to pick up condoms before knocking on her door.

She held her breath and listened for the sound of his returning steps. Instead, she heard water thundering into the tub. He hadn't gone after condoms. He was going to soak in Epsom salts.

If anything was going to happen tonight, she would have to initiate it. That was fair. He'd braved the first conversation, and she hadn't made that discussion easy on him.

When she pictured Michael and Jack discussing her lack of sex, she got angry all over again. But Michael was right about one thing. Jack had meant well.

He'd taken the only route he could think of to remedy a problem. He'd clumsily but effectively removed a barrier between two people who weren't getting any. And now, thanks to Jack's meddling, they had a golden opportunity to get some.

The more she thought about that, the more touched she was. Maybe Jack should have minded his own business, but he hadn't, and it was done, now. What a shame if his efforts went to waste.

Her heart began to pound as she envisioned what she was about to do. But she'd learned a valuable lesson in the past year. If she wanted something, she had to be willing to take the risk of going after it. She wanted Michael.

Putting down the paperback, she stripped off her clothes and took her silk bathrobe out of the closet. If she planned to seduce him, she would do it right. She hadn't brought many luxury items to Jackson Hole, but this emerald-green bathrobe had made the trip.

Next she took her hair out if its ponytail and fluffed it around her shoulders. A quick check in the full-length mirror on the back of her closet door told her that she looked…untamed. Her blood heated, much as it had when she'd hurled herself into the girl fight.

Except this time she wasn't flying into a rage over an insult. She was turning loose a more basic, primitive desire, one she'd kept in check, afraid the intensity would intimidate a lover. But now…there was Michael.

Leaving her room, she walked barefoot down to the bathroom. If he'd locked the door, then she'd have to rethink her plan. But the knob turned easily, and she walked right in.

Michael sat up so fast that water sloshed over the edge of the tub. "Keri! What the hell are you doing here?"

"Do you really have to ask?" She feasted her eyes on the first naked man she'd seen in quite a while. Michael was worth the wait.

His powerful chest heaved as he stared at her. She stared right back, enjoying the way drops of water clung to his dark chest hair and glittered in the overhead light. She followed the line of his damp body hair down to his navel and beyond, where his pride and joy rose from the water in a gratifying display of the lust he'd mentioned earlier.

She was glad he made no move to cover himself with

a washcloth. She might have caught him by surprise, but he was quickly adjusting to the possibilities of the situation. His eyes grew hot, burning with the same intensity that made her heart hammer.

Without taking his gaze from hers, he reached forward and pulled the plug. As the water drained away, he stood, his body glistening with water and radiating sexual power. He stepped out of the tub and surveyed her green robe. "Is that silk?"

"Yes."

"Unless you want to get it wet, you'd better take it off." His voice was tight, as if he was holding on to his control with difficulty.

Her blood pounded hot through her veins. "We have to get the condoms."

"Right behind you."

She turned, and there was the box, sitting on the counter. "Were you so sure of me, then?"

"No. Not sure at all. I never thought you'd come in here."

"Didn't you?"

He swallowed as his glance raked over her. "Only in my fantasies."

"We can go back to your room."

"I don't think so." Hooking a finger in her robe's sash, he pulled it free. "We're staying here."

8

TALK ABOUT WHIPLASH. He'd given up on getting any response from her tonight. He'd told himself that most women would want some time to think about whether they wanted to have a temporary fling with a guy they'd just met.

Apparently he'd misjudged. She'd walked right in on him as if she had every right in the world to do so. Damned if he was going to argue the point. No, what he had in mind was kissing her. And then…yeah, and then.

He cupped her face in both hands. God, her skin was soft. He looked into her green eyes, exactly the color of her robe. "Did some guy buy you the bathrobe?"

"No."

"Good." It shouldn't matter, but it did.

"I bought it for me. I like the feel of it on my bare skin." She slid her hands up his chest to his shoulders.

He shuddered at the caress. *Thank you, Jack.* And that was the last thought he'd give his host tonight.

He stroked his thumbs over her cheekbones. "I admire a woman who knows what she wants and goes after it."

"That's why I'm here." She clutched his shoulders. "Now kiss me before I go crazy."

"Would you really?" He leaned down and nibbled her lower lip. "I'd like that."

Her breath came in quick little gasps. "I've been known to smash crystal."

"No crystal here." He outlined her mouth with his tongue. "Do your worst." Holding off was driving him crazy, too, but it was a good kind of crazy. He didn't plan to leave this room until he'd used one of those condoms, and in the meantime, they could play.

Now that he knew the outcome, he wanted to savor the lead-up. They were two powder kegs ready to blow, and once they let loose, there would be no stopping them. This would be his only chance to build the suspense. As a bestselling author, he knew something about that.

"My worst?"

"Yeah." He feathered kisses at the corners of her mouth. "Bring it. Show me what you've got."

He wasn't even slightly prepared for what happened next. Sliding down his water-slicked body, she took his cock in her mouth. He swore softly as she reduced him to a blithering idiot. It seemed her worst was also her best.

"Enough." Somehow he found the fortitude to pull her upright before the inevitable happened. Then he gave her a long, slow and very deep kiss. She tasted of sex, and he was fast losing the battle to make this first encounter last. He wanted her wild, sassy, sexy self *now.*

But she'd thrown down a gauntlet, and any man worth his salt wouldn't ignore the challenge. Sinking to his knees, he cupped her smooth bottom and bestowed a similar, long, slow and very deep kiss on the moist cleft that was the entrance to all things wonderful.

Then he breached that entrance and reveled in her moans of pleasure. He brought her close to the edge, could almost taste victory, when she clutched his head and forced him away from paradise.

"Fair is fair." She gasped out the words, but they were clear enough. "You wouldn't let me, so I'm not letting you."

He had a good argument for why she should let him give her a climax. She could have several to his one. But if she wanted to stay even, that was okay, too. He stood and sought her mouth again. His lips were wet from all that he'd enjoyed, and she couldn't seem to get enough of kissing him.

They both became a little frantic after that. He grabbed for the condom box, but she was the one who took out the packet, tore it open and dressed him up. While she did that, he concentrated on not coming and ruining the entire enterprise.

They had a brief, breathless discussion about location, and they ended up on the floor with her on top. The floor was damn hard, and his muscles hadn't recovered from his morning ride, but once she lowered herself over his aching cock, he didn't notice or care. As she leaned over him, he finally paid proper attention to her sweet breasts, which fit exactly into his hands and tasted like wine on his lips.

She set the rhythm, and he rose to meet her as if they'd created this dance long ago. They fit together so perfectly that he found himself thinking of fate and destiny. He tried to hold her gaze, but she looked away, as if the force of this passion scared her a little.

He understood. It scared him, too. Then she pumped faster, and he forgot to be scared or even to think. There was only the pleasure, the rushing, crashing, incredible power of it driving him to lift into her, over and over.

A shred of sanity remained, enough for him to wait until he felt her convulse around him. Then he surrendered to a climax that bulldozed the breath right out of him, leaving him panting and dazed. She slumped forward, and he held her close.

As he slipped his hands under the silk of her robe to caress her warm skin, he realized she'd never taken off the robe. Its cool, smooth texture had billowed around them as they'd come together again and again, seeking their bliss. He was glad. If she kept the robe, it would always remind her of this moment.

That's when he admitted that he wouldn't be satisfied with the brief time they'd have together. He'd probably known that all along, but he'd pretended not to know. She might have done the same thing. But whether she realized it or not, he certainly did. This night had changed the game for both of them.

KERI SPENT THE night in Michael's bed, and a very fine bed it was, too. Choosing his king over her double had been a no-brainer. To make up for interrupting his soak in Epsom salts, she'd rubbed liniment into his sore muscles.

That had naturally led to a more interesting massage that resulted in another round of incredible sex. They'd both had a long day, so the addition of a couple of mind-blowing climaxes guaranteed that they'd sleep soundly, wrapped in each other's arms.

But Keri had neglected to bring her alarm clock over to Michael's room, and when she opened her eyes, the sun was up. Way up. The aroma of coffee and bacon told her that breakfast was being cooked without her. For the first time since arriving at the Last Chance, she'd overslept.

Struggling out of Michael's sleepy grip, she climbed out of bed. "I have to go."

He opened his eyes, but he wasn't fully awake. "Go where?"

"Downstairs. To my job. Mary Lou is cooking breakfast without me." She glanced at a small clock sitting on the nightstand. "Good grief. I should have been down there an hour ago!"

Michael sat up, the sheet pooling around his hips. His hair was mussed and his face was shadowed with the beginnings of a beard. He looked sexy and rumpled, the kind of man any woman would want to crawl back into bed with. "They'll make allowances," he said.

"You don't know that!" She caught a glimpse of his privileged upbringing in that statement, but she'd had a year to get over that attitude. "I doubt that Jack gave us carte blanche to ignore the ranch routine." She tied her robe with a jerk on the sash. "I'll see you later."

"Keri, wait."

"I can't. Last night was great, Michael. Really great. But I have to go." She ignored the plea in his stormy blue eyes and left the room. No matter what Jack had said, he'd still expect a day's work out of her.

Michael might see things differently, but he was a

product of the world she'd left. He was used to people *making allowances*. Once upon a time, she had been used to that, too. But she wasn't a spoiled little rich girl anymore, thank God.

Her new lifestyle had taught her to shower and dress in record time, so she was down in the kitchen in a matter of minutes. Her hair was still damp, but her clothes were clean and so was she.

Breakfast in the cozy kitchen, a meal she usually helped prepare, was in full swing. No doubt Watkins had already left for the barn, but Sarah and Pete sat at the oak table with full plates in front of them. They were involved in a deep discussion, probably something to do with the wedding. Keri could have dealt with having them there when she apologized to Mary Lou for sleeping in.

But Jack stood at the counter pouring himself a cup of coffee. She wasn't as sure that she could deal with Jack.

She met his dark gaze and caught a glint of curiosity there. She wasn't sure what he'd seen in her expression, but the corner of his mouth tilted up.

Her first impulse was to mumble some excuse and leave the room. Her second impulse was more worthy of her. She remembered that she was Keri Fitzpatrick, of the Baltimore Fitzpatricks. A Fitzpatrick didn't run and hide her head when she was caught in an awkward situation. A Fitzpatrick woman braved it out.

Her chin lifted. "Good morning, Jack."

"Morning, Keri." He smiled. "Sleep well?"

Jack Chance had *such* a devilish streak. "I did, thanks." She glanced at Mary Lou, who had turned from the stove at her entrance. Mary Lou also looked curious. "Sorry I didn't make it down in time to help you this morning, Mary Lou."

Sarah interrupted her private discussion with Pete. "Don't worry about it, Keri. I helped her. It felt good to wield a spatula again. Listen, Pete and I need everyone's opinion about the music for Saturday."

And just like that, the subject shifted away from Keri's late arrival to wedding plans. It could have been unintended, but Keri had been around Sarah Chance long enough to know that Sarah was a master at guiding social interactions into safe waters.

She wondered if Sarah had talked with Jack. Mother and son were very close, and it was always possible that Sarah had an idea of what was going on. Then again, she was extremely observant, so she might have figured things out on her own.

Pete, however, seemed oblivious. He simply followed Sarah's lead and opened up the discussion of wedding music to the group. "We planned to have Watkins play his guitar for the ceremony, but he's suggested adding the new guy, Trey Wheeler, and making it a duo. What do you think? Too much?"

Mary Lou laid down the spoon she'd been using to stir a big kettle of soup intended for lunch. "I don't think you can ever have too much guitar music. Trey and Watkins were jammin' in the kitchen the other night, and it was wonderful. Remember, Keri?"

"I do remember. I loved it. What songs are they going to play?"

"Just don't let them play 'Achy Breaky Heart.'" Jack

picked up his coffee mug and took a sip. "They purely love that tune, but it's not wedding material."

"It would be good for a laugh, though," Sarah said.

Pete leaned back in his chair. "Yeah, but are we going for laughs? How about 'I Cross My Heart'?"

"That's a good choice," Jack said. "But I don't want to get in the middle of this discussion. I'm taking my coffee and heading down to the barn." He started out of the kitchen, but then he paused. "Hey there, Michael. What's up?"

"Morning, Jack."

Keri gulped. Just when she was hoping that any potential awkwardness had been avoided, here came another dose of embarrassment through the kitchen door. She wished he'd stayed upstairs a little longer, but he hadn't, so she turned toward him with as much nonchalance as she could muster.

"Sleep well?" Jack asked oh-so-casually, repeating the question he'd put to Keri.

To Michael's credit, he didn't look at her. "Sure did. The Epsom salts and liniment did the trick."

Good Lord. Keri had to glance away and press her lips together to keep from laughing.

"Excellent news." Jack cleared his throat. "Well, I'm off to the barn. Meet me down there whenever you've finished breakfast. We'll saddle up Destiny."

"Good. Can't wait."

"That's what I like to hear. See you soon." He left the kitchen.

"Pull up a chair, Michael," Mary Lou said. "Keri, you go ahead and sit, too. There's bacon left and at least two helpings of the egg casserole Sarah and I made."

"Let me get it." Keri moved over to the stove. "You've already started lunch."

Mary Lou smiled at her. "I can wait on you this once. Go ahead and keep Michael company while he eats."

"Yes, please do," Sarah said. "Pete and I have to leave. We're driving into Jackson for some last-minute decorations, and you'll be happy to know, Keri, that we're also buying new sheets for the bunks. After two seasons of adolescent boys, we need something less worn for the wedding guests."

"New sheets would be lovely." Keri slid into the chair Michael held for her. The scent of his shaving lotion was nice, but it was the underlying aroma of liniment that stirred her the most. He must have put on more this morning. She vividly remembered helping him apply it last night, and what happened after that....

Michael nudged her knee with his, and she snapped back to the present.

Mary Lou hovered over her expectantly. "How many pieces of bacon, sweetie?"

"Two is plenty." She had a bad feeling that Mary Lou had been trying and failing to get her attention while she was daydreaming about sex with the man who currently sat right next to her. "Thank you." She directed the comment to both Michael for nudging her and Mary Lou for serving her.

Sarah tucked her napkin next to her plate and pushed back her chair. "You're looking especially pretty this morning, Keri."

"You do look great." Michael gave her a warm glance, probably warmer than he should have.

Sarah had a knowing gleam in her eye. "Maybe you should sleep in more often."

And now Keri was blushing for sure. She'd worked so hard not to get flustered, but a girl had only so much fortitude in these situations. "Thanks, but I don't like shirking my responsibilities."

"Which is laudable." Sarah rose from the table. "You've been extremely conscientious, and I appreciate that. But you and I both know this isn't a permanent career path for you."

Keri sighed. "No, it's not. I've learned so much, though. It's been good for me to have this job, in so many ways."

"A little physical work is always good for a person." Mary Lou scooped a helping of casserole onto Keri's plate. "Keeps you connected to the basics."

"That's exactly what this job has done for me," Keri said. "I wouldn't have missed the experience for the world."

"I'm glad." Sarah beamed at her before turning to Pete. "Ready?"

He drained his coffee mug and stood. "Let's do it."

"Don't forget to buy those extra chafing dishes while you're in Jackson," Mary Lou called after them. "For the wedding buffet."

"They're on the list!" Pete called back as they walked out of the kitchen.

Mary Lou glanced at Keri. "I also know you'll be leaving this job eventually, but thanks for staying through the wedding."

"Of course!"

"Normally Sarah helps when we have a big event, and I swear she'd try to do it, but we can't have that."

"No, we can't. Besides, I want to be on hand for the wedding. I'm excited for her, and for Pete. I've only known them for a year, but I feel as if it's been longer."

Mary Lou nodded. "That's the kind of people they are. They make you part of the family."

"It's a gift," Michael said. "I've only known them for a couple of days, and I already feel right at home. It'll be hard to go back to New York at the end of the week."

"Do you have to?" Mary Lou asked. "I don't think anybody needs that room in the near future, and I'm sure you'd be welcome."

"That's nice to hear, but I have to go back. There are some…some things I have to do."

"All right, then. If you must, you must. Speaking of things to be done, I have a couple of letters I was planning to write while the soup simmers, so if you'll excuse me, I'll get to it."

"By all means," Keri said. "I'll watch the soup for you."

"Thanks." Mary Lou walked back into her apartment.

After she left, the kitchen was silent except for the soft bubbling sound coming from the stove. Keri had been spared a morning-after discussion because she'd had to leave Michael's bedroom in such a rush. But she'd bet they were about to have one now.

However, they had to be careful. A normal discussion would carry into Mary Lou's apartment, but if they murmured softly, that would seem suspicious, too.

As if they'd choreographed it, they turned to each other at the same moment and started speaking.

Michael grinned, and it was the cutest expression she'd ever seen. He looked so damned happy. "You first."

"No, you." Every reservation she'd had about continuing this affair under the noses of Jack and Sarah disappeared when she saw the banked heat in his eyes, which seemed far more blue than gray this morning.

"Okay." He angled his head in the direction of Mary Lou's apartment, as if acknowledging their need for caution. "I wanted to thank you for locating the Epsom salts and the liniment for me."

"You're welcome." She winked at him. "It was my pleasure."

"You're very good at what you do."

"Thanks for the compliment." Heat sluiced through her at the look in his eyes. "It's wonderful to be appreciated."

"I plan to make a habit of the Epsom salts and liniment while I'm here."

She pressed her napkin to her mouth to keep from giggling. When she had control of herself, she leaned toward him. "I absolutely think you should. It's so good for you."

"I know." His tone became more urgent. "Sure wish I could take a treatment right now."

"But Jack's expecting you any minute."

"Yeah, he is." He scooted back his chair and picked up his plate.

"Hey, you didn't finish your breakfast."

"No." He stood and gestured to the prominent jut of his fly. "But as you can plainly see, I have to leave."

She gazed up at him. "Pity."

"Isn't it, though?" He winced as he walked over to the sink and dumped his food down the garbage disposal. "If I had time for a treatment, I might not have so much trouble walking right now."

"Think about Destiny. That'll take your mind off your problem."

He turned back to her. "The horse or the concept?"

"I meant the horse."

"I was hoping you meant the concept. I don't think it's an accident that we both ended up at this ranch together."

"Michael, I—"

"Gotta go. See you at lunch." He walked slowly and deliberately out of the kitchen.

She sat there staring at the empty doorway. Maybe he'd come back, pop his head in and say *just kidding*. But he didn't, and she was left with the conviction that he'd jumped way past this week and was already planning a reunion once they were both on the east coast.

If so, she needed to let him know that she wouldn't be living there from now on. She didn't want him building castles in the air. He was a storyteller, so he might be prone to that.

But damn, he'd looked so happy this morning. She hated to burst his bubble. But as she'd concluded last night, she wasn't a city girl anymore.

9

WHEN MICHAEL ARRIVED at the barn, Jack had already mounted a black-and-white Paint, one that was smaller than Bandit and didn't have the eye patches. Destiny was tied to the hitching post by his lead rope.

Jack walked his horse toward Michael. "Go get Destiny tacked up. We're heading out today."

Michael squinted as he looked up at Jack, who was wearing his shades again. Michael had pricey sunglasses in his room, but he hadn't worn them. He figured they'd fly off his face and get crunched in the dirt within the first five minutes of bouncing around on Destiny.

This morning, though, he wished he'd worn them, after all. Jack would have a harder time reading him if he had on shades. "Am I ready for that?"

Jack grinned. Despite his dark glasses, there was no mistaking the mischief in his expression. "You tell me. If you're too exhausted from your night's activities, we can always—"

"I'll saddle Destiny." Michael lengthened his stride

as he headed for the barn. Now that his erection had subsided, he moved damned well, if he said so himself.

He'd made a joke out of how much the liniment had helped, but apparently it had. Either that or great sex loosened up a guy's muscles better than anything else. He was more than willing to believe that.

Jack had left him alone to saddle and bridle Destiny, which he appreciated. After practicing so many times yesterday, he remembered what to do. Accomplishing it by himself and swinging up in the saddle made him feel like a semi-proficient rider.

Once Destiny started to move, though, he discovered a few twinges that hadn't bothered him until now. Yeah, he was saddle sore. Not incapacitated, though.

Jack rode up beside him. "Nice work."

"Thanks. Which horse is that?"

"This here's Ink Spot. Bandit's not up to a trail ride yet, so I'm giving this boy some exercise. How're you feeling?"

Michael nodded. "Good."

"You're looking good, too. More relaxed and loose. I always say there's nothing like a—"

"Jack, I don't want to talk about it."

That typical Jack grin appeared again. "You don't have to say another word, buddy. But just know that I'm happy for you."

"So we can drop the subject?"

"Absolutely. I can tell by the look on your face that you're a very satisfied man this morning. No discussion necessary."

"Glad to hear it. Now let's—"

"And Keri looked like a very satisfied woman, too."

"Jack, for God's sake."

"Just making a comment."

Michael sighed and waved a hand at Jack. "Okay, you're obviously very proud of yourself and need to have your say. Go ahead."

"Matter of fact, I am proud of myself, and I'll tell you why."

"I'm sure you will. Just don't get graphic or I'll have to punch you, and then I'd probably fall off this horse."

"Nothing graphic on my mind. Just an observation." Jack rested both hands on the saddle horn and sat back, almost as if he'd taken a spot in one of the porch rocking chairs. "When I met you at the airport, you were a man living in his head. I can imagine why that is. You're a writer, so a lot goes on in that head of yours."

Michael adopted Jack's posture, hands resting on the saddle horn, butt sitting easy on the saddle. It felt… right, as if he was supposed to be sitting in that saddle talking to Jack on this bright August morning.

"The thing is," Jack continued, "to be a cowboy, you have to live in your body, too. Riding is great for that. But good sex is even better. In fact, the two have some things in common. You have to feel the motion of the horse when you're riding the same way you sense the motion of a woman when you're making love to her." He paused and looked at Michael. "Your jaw's kind of tight. Is that too graphic for you?"

"You're skating on the edge, my friend." But Michael understood exactly what Jack was saying, and he was right. Having a vivid imagination was both a blessing and a curse. Michael could conjure up stories like nobody's business, but sometimes he forgot to come down from the clouds and experience reality.

"That's about all I had to say, anyway." Jack sat up straighter and gathered the reins in one hand. "I'll make a prediction, though. You'll find being on the back of a horse a much easier proposition today, and not only because of the practice in the corral yesterday." He clucked to Ink Spot. "Let's ride."

Michael hoped that prediction would be true, but when Destiny broke into a trot, he bounced the way he had before. He thought about what Jack had said, and then he thought about the effortless way he and Keri had moved together in the king-sized bed.

There had been nothing intellectual about that experience. They'd communicated on a purely physical level as they explored different rhythms and found the one that worked. Wow, had it worked.

The heated memory of what he'd shared with Keri cushioned the jolting discomfort of Destiny's trot. And sometime later, Michael realized he wasn't bouncing anymore. Instead, he was moving with the motion of the horse. His body knew what to do if he stopped trying to think his way through the problem.

Once he could relax and enjoy the ride, he paid attention to his surroundings. Dry grass warmed by the sun smelled faintly like the old books in his family's library. They rode past a stand of evergreens, and he picked up the crisp scent of pine and the warble of songbirds flitting among the branches. The creak of leather and the steady beat of hooves had a lulling effect.

Across the meadow, the snow-topped Grand Tetons rose against a blue sky. A hawk wheeled overhead, probably searching for breakfast. No wait, that wasn't a hawk. Michael shaded his eyes and looked up. White feathered head, big wingspan. A bald eagle.

Michael looked at Jack ahead of him on the trail. Jack was watching the eagle, too.

"Do you see many of those?" Michael called out.

"We have a pair of them nesting on the edge of the property. A woman named Naomi Perkins is camped out there while she studies them. That could be one of them. I'm sure there are others in the area, too."

"I've only seen pictures of them." Michael had expected to see wildlife while he was out here. He hadn't expected to be dazzled by it. He watched the eagle until it was only a speck in the sky.

Meanwhile Destiny, who'd picked up on the fact that Michael wasn't paying attention to him, had stopped to munch on the dry grass beside the trail.

Jack was several yards ahead of them by now. He turned in the saddle. "Pull his head up. Don't let him eat like that." Jack continued along at a good clip.

"Right." But Destiny was a deeply stubborn animal who wouldn't give up his snack easily. By the time Michael wrestled him away from the grass, Jack was more like thirty yards away.

Nudging Destiny's belly with his heels, Michael clucked at the horse the way Jack did when he wanted to get the animal moving. Destiny's ears pricked forward and he seemed to notice for the first time that he was lagging behind.

Michael nudged him again, and a quick walk turned into a trot. They weren't catching up, though, so Michael made that clucking sound to speed up the process.

Destiny surged forward in a rolling gait that covered the ground much faster. After the first shock of the faster pace, Michael discovered he *loved* it. He didn't know if they were galloping or not, but this was how he wanted to ride, rocking gently in the saddle with the wind in his face.

Jack turned in the saddle, flashed a quick grin, and took Ink Spot's speed up to match Destiny's. "How do you like cantering?" he called over his shoulder.

"This is cantering? I thought we were galloping."

"Nope. Galloping is much faster, and we won't be doing that." Jack slowed Ink Spot to a trot, and finally to a walk. "We'll head back now, and walk them in." He turned Ink Spot in a semicircle, cutting through the grass to head back the same way.

"Works for me." Michael guided Destiny along the same route and paid attention so Destiny didn't pause to chew on grass now that they were moving so slowly.

Jack regained the trail and swiveled in his saddle. "Congratulations, cowboy. You've ridden a trot and a canter. It wasn't always pretty, but you stayed on. I think by the time you leave you'll be good enough to fool them during the video."

"I guess." Michael had forgotten all about the filming. He'd been immersed in this experience for its own sake, testing himself to see if he could hack it. So far, he'd done okay. And this was only Wednesday, his second full day of lessons. He might have the makings of a cowboy, after all.

"You know what?" he said. "Let's not worry too much about what skills I need for the video. Just teach me everything you can in the time we have."

Jack pivoted in the saddle again. "You want to learn how to pen cattle?"

Two days ago, Michael would have been too intimidated to even try something like that. But that was two days ago. "Do you have time to teach me?"

"I can show you some of the basics. I can't turn you into an expert in two days, but the cutting horse does most of the work, anyway. We can start this afternoon, and we'll have all day tomorrow. You'll get the idea."

"Then yes, I'd like that."

"All righty." Jack smiled. "After you get comfortable with it, like maybe tomorrow afternoon, you should invite Keri down to watch. It impresses the hell out of women."

"That wouldn't be my motivation, Jack."

"Maybe not, but when it comes to the ladies, a cowboy uses all his tools."

DURING LUNCH, KERI noticed that Michael seemed more relaxed around the other cowhands. His riding lesson with Jack this morning seemed to have gone well, judging from the way Michael was joking around with everyone. Yesterday he'd seemed worried that he wouldn't make the grade, but he'd gained confidence in the past twenty-four hours.

She couldn't help wondering if his high spirits came partly from his new relationship with her. She hoped not. His remark about destiny bringing them together continued to worry her. They might need to have a discussion about that tonight, just to make sure they understood each other before they got in any deeper.

Thinking about what else might happen tonight made

her hot and bothered, so she shoved those thoughts away. When Michael said hello, she returned his greeting with a casual smile. Jack might know what was going on, but the rest of the crew didn't need to find out. They probably wouldn't, though, because everyone was focused on the upcoming wedding on Saturday.

Keri couldn't believe it was Wednesday already. She had the upstairs in good shape, though. Once Sarah and Pete brought home the new sheets, she'd make up the beds for the wedding guests, who were mostly Pete's friends.

Meanwhile the ranch hands were making minor repairs to the barn and the corrals so the place would look perfect by Friday afternoon. On Saturday they'd set up the tents and the dancing platform for the outdoor reception. The wedding itself would be held in the ranch house living room.

Keri wouldn't be in charge of creating that venue. Jack's sister-in-law Tyler Keller was a professional party planner, and she in turn would get plenty of help from Sarah's daughters-in-law when it came time to decorate. Keri just had to make sure the area stayed clean.

That reminded her that Sarah had asked for every last bit of soot to be cleaned out of the fireplace, because they planned to fill the cavity with greenery and flowers. As she helped Mary Lou clear the lunch dishes, she asked for some tips on how to do it.

"Don't use the regular vacuum cleaner," Mary Lou said. "Let me go get the old wet/dry vac from the laundry room." She set down a load of dishes and left the kitchen. In a few moments she was back with the canister and a hose. "Go ahead and get started. I can finish up here."

"Okay."

"And change out of that white shirt. You're going to get filthy. Do you have something old to wear?"

Keri paused to think.

"Never mind. I have an old shirt you can put on. I use it whenever we repaint." She left again and returned with a button-up shirt covered in paint splatters of various colors. "It's ugly, but it's clean."

"Thanks, Mary Lou." Keri took the shirt and the vacuum cleaner and left the kitchen. Michael and Jack and a few of the hands were still in the dining room, and as Keri walked by she heard enough of the conversation to gather they were talking about cutting horses.

That made sense. The Last Chance was famous for their well-trained cutting horses. She'd watched a demonstration this summer and had found the maneuvers fascinating but tricky. She doubted that Michael was up to that kind of riding yet, but maybe he planned to watch someone else do it.

After dropping off the vacuum in the living room, she climbed the stairs to the second floor. In her room, she pulled off her white T-shirt and put on Mary Lou's shirt. It hung on her, but that didn't matter.

As she started out of her room again, she heard boots on the stairs. Adrenaline sent her heart racing—only one person had a reason to come up here.

Michael topped the stairs and came down the hallway toward her. "Interesting outfit."

"It's Mary Lou's shirt." Her breath hitched at the heat in his eyes. "I'm going to clean out the fireplace."

"I wondered. I went looking for you and found the vacuum cleaner, but you were gone. I decided to see if you were up here."

"You were looking for me? Why?" Silly question. His expression told her exactly why.

"Because I was going crazy all through lunch." He stepped closer. "I needed this." He drew her into his arms.

She told herself that she should resist, but being held in those strong arms felt like heaven. "I'm not sure we should—"

"Just one kiss. I have to get down to the barn. Jack's going to start teaching me how to ride a cutting horse."

"He is? Listen, be careful. That's tricky."

"That's why I want to learn." His head dipped. "I like tricky."

Well, she liked *this*—his warm, clever mouth seducing her, his tongue teasing her with promises of what he'd do to her later tonight, his hand slipping under the hem of the loose shirt to cup her breast….

Before she realized what he had in mind, he'd flipped open the front catch of her bra and was stroking her nipple with his thumb. His kiss deepened, and he pulled her against the hard ridge of his penis.

Now she *really* should resist. But instead of pushing him away, she'd somehow shoved her hands in the back pockets of his jeans and urged him even closer.

His kiss turned from a full-on assault to soft nibbles. "If I don't let you go right now, I'm going to drag you into my bedroom and strip you naked."

She gulped for air. "That would be bad. You'd never hear the end of it from Jack."

"That's for sure." He squeezed her breast. "But it would almost be worth it."

She forced herself to slip her hands from his pockets. "Let me go, Michael." Her voice didn't carry much conviction. "I'll see you tonight."

He groaned and leaned his forehead against hers. "That's hours away."

"But then we'll have hours together." She rested her palms on his chest and felt the wild beat of his heart. If she pushed gently he'd probably release her, but she couldn't make herself do it. His warmth made her want to nestle closer, not pull away.

"Okay, I'm going to be strong." Drawing in a shaky breath, he stepped back and gazed at her, his eyes the blue-gray of storm clouds. "I'll be upstairs as soon as I can possibly get away tonight."

"Me, too." She trembled, still not in control of her impulses. "I think Sarah knows."

"I think so, too, but she doesn't seem to disapprove. If anything, she seems happy about it."

"Well, she won't be if I start slacking off." She said that as much to remind herself as to inform Michael.

He took another deep breath. "And I have to get down to the barn." Reaching out, he brushed a finger over her cheek. "See you tonight."

"It's a date." She waited until he'd started down the stairs before she reached under the shirt and hooked her bra in place.

Her body was moist and achy from his touch, and she was honest enough to admit that if he'd tried to maneuver her back to his bedroom, she'd probably have

FREE Merchandise is 'in the Cards' for you!

Dear Reader,

We're giving away FREE MERCHANDISE!

Seriously, we'd like to reward you for reading this novel by giving you **FREE MERCHANDISE** worth over $20. And no purchase is necessary!

You see the Jack of Hearts sticker above? Paste that sticker in the box on the Free Merchandise Voucher inside. Return the Voucher promptly...and we'll send you valuable Free Merchandise!

Thanks again for reading one of our novels—and enjoy your Free Merchandise with our compliments!

Pam Powers

Pam Powers

P.S. Look inside to see what Free Merchandise is **"in the cards"** for you!

HB-FM-08/13

W

e'd like to send you two free books to introduce you to the Harlequin® Blaze™ series. These books are worth over $10, but they are yours to keep absolutely FREE! We'll even send you 2 wonderful surprise gifts. You can't lose!

REMEMBER: Your Free Merchandise, consisting of **2 Free Books** and **2 Free Gifts**, is worth over $20.00! No purchase is necessary, so please send for your Free Merchandise today.

YOUR FREE MERCHANDISE INCLUDES...

2 FREE Harlequin® Blaze™ Books
AND 2 FREE Mystery Gifts

FREE MERCHANDISE VOUCHER

Please send my Free Merchandise, consisting of
2 Free Books and **2 Free Mystery Gifts**.
I understand that I am under no obligation to buy
anything, as explained on the back of this card.

150/350 HDL F42D

Please Print

FIRST NAME

LAST NAME

ADDRESS

APT.#   CITY

STATE/PROV.   ZIP/POSTAL CODE

NO PURCHASE NECESSARY!

▲ Detach card and mail today. No stamp needed. ▲

© 2013 HARLEQUIN ENTERPRISES LIMITED. ® and ™ are trademarks owned and used by the trademark owner and/or its licensee. Printed in the U.S.A.

HB-FM-08/13

let him do it. He tempted the hot-blooded Irish lass she kept hidden most of the time. When that side of her cut loose, no telling what might happen.

10

MICHAEL HAD TROUBLE sitting through dinner with Sarah and Pete that night. And it wasn't only because he was eager to get upstairs and be with Keri. He ached all over, and the longer he sat, the more his muscles stiffened. In his zeal to practice riding a cutting horse, he'd stayed in the saddle way too long this afternoon.

He'd admitted to a few aches and pains, and Pete had been generous with the Scotch. The liquor had helped, but he still hurt. He hoped to hell his enthusiasm for riding hadn't ruined what promised to be another night of great sex.

When dinner was over, he winced as he rose from the table.

Sarah noticed. "I recommend a long soak in Epsom salts," she said. "And tomorrow you need to tell Jack to ease up on you."

"Jack's not to blame." Michael hobbled to the doorway. "I'm the damned fool who wanted to stay out there. I was having fun and didn't realize what I was doing to myself."

"I'm glad to hear you were having fun, at least."

Sarah gave him a sympathetic smile. "Epsom salts, plenty of liniment and a good night's sleep. You'll be better in the morning."

"I'm sure I will be. See you both for breakfast." He made his way down the hall and climbed the stairs with effort. He knew Keri wouldn't be in her room yet. If the meal had just ended, Keri would be helping Mary Lou with the cleanup.

That was okay with him. He'd soak in the tub and hope that it restored him to vibrant manliness. He wanted to be a tiger in bed tonight, but at the moment he felt like a slightly drunk pussycat.

Not long afterward, he slipped into the warm, salted water with a groan. Yes, this was going to help. He put a rolled-up towel behind his neck and slid as far into the water as he could, considering the length of the tub and his six-two frame.

Closing his eyes, he drifted in the soothing water and his tortured muscles stopped screaming at him. He didn't want to go to sleep, but the combination of the warm water and the lingering effects of the Scotch tugged at him. Maybe just a little nap....

The water had cooled by the time he slowly came awake. But that wasn't what had roused him from sleep. Although he lay still, the water rippled around him, and something wonderful was happening to his cock. So nice. He hated to open his eyes, in case he was dreaming the sweet massage and opening his eyes would make it stop.

But the pressure felt real, and finally he looked. Keri, without a stitch on, knelt by the tub, one arm braced on the edge and the other hand lazily stroking his very happy johnson. She gazed at his growing erection with interest, as if conducting a scientific experiment.

"Having fun?"

Her glance shifted to his face, and her green eyes were lit with the passion he longed to see there. "You're awake."

"Some parts more than others."

She kept toying with him. "The water's getting cold. Cold water won't help much. You need to change the water, or—"

"Do something with what you're building there?" He checked out the stiff evidence and figured he was more than ready to party.

"I don't want to put a strain on you. Sarah mentioned you were in bad shape." But her fondling continued, and the flame danced in her eyes.

"I'm in terrible shape. I need you to keep that up for a really long time."

"Michael, be serious. Are you hurting?"

"Yeah. My nuts ache like you wouldn't believe."

The corners of her mouth tipped up. "I could just keep doing this and relieve the pressure."

"To hell with that." He sat up and discovered that the pain was still there, but not nearly as bad. The potential explosion threatening in the region of his groin, however, was a more urgent matter.

Her forehead creased in a cute little frown. "Think you can make it to the bedroom?"

"Probably not. Did you happen to bring a condom in with you?"

"Well…yes." She gestured toward the counter. "I left it over there."

"That's my girl. Stand back. I'm getting out." As he navigated out of the tub with some decent dexterity but a few moans and groans thrown in, he could tell she was trying not to laugh. "It's okay," he said. "You're allowed to make fun of me. It was my own stupid fault."

She handed him a towel. "I think you're brave. I admire a man who goes all out."

"You do?" He tossed the towel aside. "Then you're going to love this." He grabbed her and lifted her to the counter so abruptly that she squealed. That gratified him. He didn't relish playing the role of the invalid.

Dropping to his knees sent shooting pains through his body, but he ignored them. The reward for doing it would be worth whatever it cost him. "Prop your hands behind you."

"Michael, I don't know if you should…" Her protest died away as he settled her knees over his shoulders, cupped her bottom and drew her gently to the edge of the vanity.

Her sigh was deep and heartfelt. "Oh, Michael. Michael, that's…good." After that, words seemed to fail her as her moans of delight blended with the liquid sound of his tongue and his mouth as he feasted on her many treasures.

She didn't yell when she came, which was a good thing because he didn't know how well sound carried in this house. But she arched against him and moaned his name low in her throat as the spasms rocked her.

Heart pounding with triumph, he licked the juices heated by her passion. Her passion for *him*. She'd said his name. She knew who knelt between her thighs and sought her essence.

When he stood, he clenched his jaw against a cry of pain. But his throbbing cock demanded satisfaction. He found the condom she'd left on the counter and put it on.

She watched him, leaning back on her hands, her eyes heavy-lidded in the aftermath of her climax, her body limp, pliable. Lust pumped through him like molten lava, urging him to take her with abandon. Grasping her ankles, he lifted them to his shoulders.

Her eyes widened.

"Yes." He gazed down at her, so open, so vulnerable. She wouldn't be able to move. But he could. "Just like this." And he shoved in deep, lifting her off the vanity.

She gasped.

He wanted to take her, but he didn't want to hurt her. "Keri, did I—"

"No!" She began to pant, softly, seductively. "No, it's good. It's good. Don't stop."

That was all he needed to know. He grasped her bottom to keep her steady and began to thrust. Dear God. This was intense. He looked into her eyes, and saw his own raw hunger reflected there.

He pumped faster, and she began to whimper. Faster yet, and she let out a high, keening cry. He no longer cared who could hear as he drove into her again and again. He felt her tighten around his cock. Then she came, breathing hard, and he rocketed forward, seeking, seeking, and finding…yes…*yes*. With a groan he sank forward, into her, as his cock pulsed in a glorious, liberating rhythm.

He stayed braced against her for several long seconds as he slowly recovered from the rocket-ship ride of making love to Keri Fitzpatrick. As a guy with an imagination, he'd harbored quite a few sexual fantasies. He had a feeling she could make every single one of them come true.

DESPITE MICHAEL'S AMAZING performance in the bathroom, Keri was worried that he'd end up crippled by tomorrow if he didn't slow down. When they finally made it into his big bed, she insisted on massaging him with liniment. He made some mild protest about feeling like a damned baby, but he stretched out on his stomach with a sigh of relief.

By the light from the bedside lamp, she worked the cream into his muscles, which gave her the perfect excuse to admire his body. He might be a writer, but he had the physique of an athlete. His broad shoulders tapered to slim hips and a sculpted backside. His thighs and calves had the definition of a runner.

"Where did you get all these muscles?" she asked as she worked on his back with her fingertips and the heels of both hands.

"Gym membership. Didn't prepare me for this, though."

"Horseback riding is its own thing." She scooted down and began massaging his thighs.

"No kidding." He moaned softly.

"Am I hurting you?"

"Not really. It feels good, in an intense sort of way." He inhaled slowly and exhaled even more slowly, as if breathing through the pain. "Do you ride?"

"Yes, if I have time. When the boys are here, I'm usually busy with them and don't ride much. Part of my job was teaching them to clean up after themselves."

"Did they learn?"

"They got better at it."

"Maybe you need to teach me."

"Nah." She used firm strokes on his calves. "You're an honored guest."

"Everybody else works on the ranch. I feel like a spoiled rich guy."

"You're not so bad." She moved back up to his thigh muscles. She guessed those needed the most attention from the way he'd moaned earlier. "You hung up your towels and picked up your clothes."

"But I didn't make my bed."

"No." She smoothed her hand up over the swell of his butt. Nice buns. "But I liked doing that. It reminded me of all the fun we had."

"Maybe we should make the bed together, so we can both enjoy those memories."

"You know perfectly well that we'd never get it done." Somehow her massage had turned into a caress. He really did have spectacular butt cheeks.

"So were you turned on by making my bed?"

"Maybe." She was getting turned on now, that was for sure.

"Did you stretch out on it and wish I could be there, buried deep inside you?"

"It's possible I did, just for a moment."

His voice roughened. "Did thinking about that make you wet and achy?"

"Yes." Giving in to temptation, she leaned down and kissed his firm butt. Not satisfied with that, she licked the spot, and kissed him again.

"You do realize you're driving me insane when you do that."

"I hope so." She kissed the other side. "Because I really want to make another memory in this bed right now."

"How convenient." He rolled away from her and gestured toward his penis, which stood at rigid attention. "Apparently, so do I."

Things moved quickly after that. She soon found herself on her back looking into Michael's beautiful eyes as he aligned his body with hers.

"I'll suit up in a minute," he murmured. "Once I put that condom on I'm like one of Pavlov's dogs. I have to go for it. But first I want to take some time to just look at you." He rubbed his chest lightly over her breasts and lifted up so he could see his handiwork. "I like it when your nipples perk up and take notice."

"Me, too." She took a quick breath. "I like it when you suck on them."

His gaze grew hot. "Is that a request?"

"Well, as long as you're looking, you might as well sample what I have to offer."

"What an excellent idea." As he slid farther down, he made plenty of skin-to-skin contact. Braced above her, he focused on her breasts. "So perfect. I can't decide which to taste first. Choose for me, Mistress Keri."

Heat surged through her as she cupped her right breast and lifted it toward him. "This one, if you please, kind sir."

"I would be most pleased." Dipping his head, he kissed the very tip of her nipple. Then he swirled his tongue around it. And again, a fleeting caress.

"More." Her throaty plea came unbidden.

"Ah, Keri." Leaning down, he opened his mouth and closed it over her nipple. His cheeks hollowed as he drew her in.

She felt the tug all the way to her womb. Using his tongue to increase the pressure, he began a rhythmic sucking motion, and her body clenched in response. She arched against him, wanting....

As if in answer to her unspoken need, he shifted his weight to one arm and reached between her thighs. His touch was smooth, gliding in on a rush of moisture.

Yes. She moaned as his fingers worked their magic. So good. So very...with a gasp of surprise, she came, the tremors rolling through her in quick succession as she gulped for air.

He lifted his head from her breast and gazed into her eyes. His hand slowed to a gentle, easy rhythm, and he smiled. "Again, Keri. I want to watch this time."

Her body was his to command. She spontaneously tightened around his fingers and lifted her hips.

"That's it," he murmured, deepening his caress. "You're so beautiful like this, with your breasts all rosy and your eyes getting darker the closer you get." His breathing roughened. "I could almost come, just looking at you."

His intensity turned his eyes to a deep gray. She was mesmerized by the heat in those eyes as he probed the very core of her sexual being.

"But I won't come." He stroked her with deliberate intent. "I'd rather watch you. Now you're closer yet. I can feel it right there." He thrust his fingers deep again.

She began to whimper.

"Soon, Keri, soon. I can see the climax in your eyes. I can feel it in your body. Almost there. Now, Keri. Now!" He pumped faster.

She erupted, lifting off the bed with a cry of surrender. Murmuring words of encouragement, he continued to pleasure her until she sank back, dragging in air and drained of every ounce of tension.

She closed her eyes and savored the gift he'd given her. Then she opened them and gazed up at him. "That was…amazing."

"For me, too."

She took a shaky breath and reached to stroke his cheek. "But I'll bet you're about ready to die of frustration."

"Pretty much." His voice sounded strained.

"Then let's do something about that. Lie back and let me take care of you for a change."

"I hope you're not talking about liniment."

That made her smile. "No." She brushed her fingertips over his chin, darkened with the beginnings of a beard. It made him look a little dangerous and a lot sexy. She ran her tongue over her lips. "I have a different therapy in mind."

11

MICHAEL DIDN'T THINK there was a man alive who could resist a woman who offered to give him a tongue bath. She licked him from stem to stern, with her dark hair curtaining her face and tickling his skin. He hadn't realized that his nipples were so sensitive, or the inside of his elbow, or the spaces between his toes.

The experience was erotic as hell, probably even more so because she didn't lay her tongue or a finger on his extremely erect cock. He just prayed he could hold himself together long enough for her to reach that pivotal point. She had to go there eventually.

In the meantime, she made him moan, and gasp and sweat. If she kept avoiding the main event, she was going to make him beg. Maybe that was the idea.

He struggled to catch his breath. "Keri?"

"Mmm?" From her position down at his feet, she looked up the length of his body. She had to peer around his stiff rod to make eye contact.

"Are you going to…"

She smiled. "Yes, Michael, I am."

"When?"

"I wanted to build the suspense so it would be super good."

He nearly choked. "If you build it any higher, I'll be able to break bricks with my cock."

"Well, then." She did a little maneuver that allowed her to settle her plump breasts on his shins. "I'll move to the next phase." She slid up his body with a maddening lack of haste, but at last she lay with her breasts cradled against his thighs and her warm breath against his shaft.

His pulse rate skyrocketed. She adjusted her position, and one of her nipples grazed his balls. He almost came from that alone. Gritting his teeth, he fought back the orgasm that prowled like a tiger in a cage.

She kissed the base of his cock. He wanted to see, but he was afraid the visual would do him in. Ah, hell. He was nearly a goner, anyway. Stuffing a pillow behind his head, he looked down to where she lay. From that position, she'd never be able to carry out the job he had in mind for that full mouth of hers.

He started to make a suggestion, but before he could, she braced her forearms on the bed and began to glide upward. As she rose, she flattened her tongue against the ridged underside of his penis. He groaned and fisted his hands in the sheet. He wouldn't come, he wouldn't come, he wouldn't come.

He didn't, but it was a close call. A drop of moisture trembled on the tip. When she reached that point, she licked it off, and he groaned again, a little louder this time.

Meeting his gaze, she winked at him.

"You're a devil." He sounded as if he'd swallowed barbed wire.

"This is for your own good." Then she finally, *finally* closed her mouth over his johnson. But she wasn't finished with him yet. Circling the base with her thumb and forefinger, she created the equivalent of a cock ring.

He'd had a vague idea of the concept, but she showed him exactly how it worked. She drove him into a frenzy with her tongue, her lips, even her teeth. When she knew he was about to come, she squeezed the base of his penis until his breathing slowed a little. And then she took him back up again—and again.

He went a little nuts—laughing, moaning, writhing against the mattress—until the moment she let go and took him in all the way to the back of her throat with the strongest suction she'd used so far. His climax roared through him with the force of a tsunami. He came, and came and came.

She took it all. As he gasped for air and stared at the ceiling, he heard her swallow. That, he thought, had to be the most intimate bedroom sound in the world. He was one lucky sonofabitch to be here with Keri listening to her swallow like that. At this moment, he wouldn't trade places with any guy, anywhere, not even someone dominating the bestseller charts.

CUDDLING AFTER SPECTACULAR sex rated high on Keri's list, and fortunately, Michael also seemed to be a fan.

"I don't want to fall asleep, though." He gathered her against him, spoon fashion.

"You should sleep." Snuggling into the warm curve of his body, she felt relaxed and cozy. She'd planned for falling asleep in his bed this time. Before her little ambush in the tub, she'd left her cell phone on his bedside table and had set the alarm. "You'll have another big day tomorrow."

"Yeah, but I'm having a big night tonight." He wrapped his arm around her and cupped her breast. "That's more important to me than my big day tomorrow."

"Uh-oh." Guilt washed over her. "Am I distracting you from what you came out here to do?"

"Nope." He lazily fondled her breast. "You're helping."

"Maybe a little bit, by rubbing liniment on you, but you could do that for yourself, and you'd get more sleep without me around."

"No, I wouldn't. I'd know you were right across the hall and I'd lie awake with a stiff cock all night."

"Yes, but we've taken care of that. Twice, in fact. Much as I love being here in your bed, I should probably go back to my own room." She started to pull away.

His grip tightened. "Don't you dare leave, especially out of guilt. You're the reason I rode so well this morning, so stop thinking you're a hindrance. Jack predicted I'd do better after having good sex, and—"

"Wait a minute. Jack recommended going to bed with me because it would make you a better rider? Now I'm insulted!" She tried harder to squirm away, but he held her fast.

"No, he didn't do that. Stop struggling and check your Irish temper for a second, okay?"

"This better be good." She relaxed against him again, because it was what she really wanted to do, anyway.

"Oh, it is good." He loosened his hold and kissed her shoulder. "Win-win. Jack said I had to get out of my head and into my body if I wanted to learn to ride well. Yesterday I couldn't do that, but after being with you last night, I got much better at it." He cupped her breast again. "Sex with you keeps me grounded."

"That's nice to hear, but let's get back to the part where Jack predicted your riding would improve after having sex with me. When did he say that?"

"Ah, I see what the problem is. You think he said that yesterday and that's why he wanted us to get together."

"Well, isn't it?"

"No. Okay, maybe a little bit, but that was an afterthought, I'm sure. He didn't make that remark about sex helping horsemanship until this morning, after he figured out we'd had a fun time last night."

"I'm not sure I believe it helps all that much. He might be trying to justify this arrangement."

"Oh, it helps. You know how we just instinctively move in rhythm with each other during sex?"

"Yeah." And talking about it was getting her hot. She didn't think that was possible after all they'd done tonight, but she couldn't deny the tension coiling within her.

"I had to let my body feel the rhythm of the horse and go with it. I was thinking about you, and how great we felt together, and suddenly I was sitting a trot without bouncing."

"Huh. That's cool." Keri sighed and nestled closer to his warmth. "Okay, I feel better now."

"Actually, you feel outstanding." He stroked her breast. "Silky soft. I love touching you."

"FYI, touching me is producing certain results. I'm not saying we should do anything about it, but—"

"But we could." He nudged her with his growing erection. "Incredibly enough."

"I know." She pressed against him, reveling in her power to arouse him again. "I hope we don't kill each other with too much sex."

"If we do, I'll die a happy man." He slid his hand between her thighs. "Mmm. I think you're ready for another round."

"Told you." She started to turn toward him.

"Stay there. Stay right…there." And he withdrew his hand.

She missed his caress, but she was eager to find out exactly what he had in mind. Cool air wafted over her as he moved away.

Foil crinkled, latex snapped and he was back. "I want to try it like this, on our sides." He grasped her hips, angled his body and eased into her from behind. "I couldn't do this, except you are so…wet." He moved slowly until he was deep inside. His breathing came faster, now. "How's that?"

"Different." She hadn't thought she was a fan of this position, but now that he was there, filling her, she thought she might like it, after all. And he seemed to love it.

He cradled her breast, as before, but now they were intimately connected as he lightly pinched her nipple. His fingers began a rhythmic kneading motion as he began to move within her. He was slow at first, almost careful.

But then he stroked faster, and the world shifted. Having sex like this was a step away from civilization and a step toward primitive lust. She felt it, and judging from the energy he put into each thrust, he felt it, too.

From this angle, her passage was narrower, which meant she felt the slide of his penis more intensely. Surely he did, too, which would explain his ragged breathing and his eagerness to pound into her over and over. She trembled on the edge of a climax that drew nearer each time he drove forward. Then he released his hold on her hip to reach around and slip his finger into her cleft. He pressed down, and she came in a rush amid wild cries of completion.

He kept his hand there, steadying her as he plunged into her with abandon until he shuddered against her, moaning softly, holding her tight to receive all that he had to give. Their breathing slowed, and they lay still, coupled together in an ancient posture.

She'd never before felt taken, but she felt it now. She and Michael were knocking down the barriers between them one by one. With each barrier that fell, they became more vulnerable to being hurt when they eventually had to part.

And they would part. His life was in New York, in the heart of the publishing world, while hers, once she handled some details in Baltimore, would be in Jackson Hole. If she had any sense, she'd pull back. She'd protect herself and protect him, too, from risking too much.

But being with Michael was so good. And he'd said that she was helping him become a better cowboy. That was all the rationalization she needed for indulging in sexual pleasure the likes of which she'd never known.

LATER, MICHAEL LAY on his back beside Keri. They held hands but they didn't speak, almost as if they both needed time to process what was going on. He couldn't be certain of her state of mind, but his was certainly on tilt.

He'd never experienced intimacy like this. The reason was obvious. He'd known this might happen before they'd begun the affair. He'd finally gotten naked with a woman emotionally as well as physically. Until now, no lover had truly known him, known the wildness deep in his soul. He wasn't sure if it was Keri or the ranch, or maybe the combination of the two that brought it out.

Because of that, he wasn't sure he could trust his feelings for her. He thought they might have a future, but what if the dynamic changed once they were both living back east? Would he be the same uninhibited person if they met up in New York? Would she?

She gave his hand a squeeze. "I have a question for you."

"Shoot." Considering the direction of his thoughts, questions made his heart thump a little faster. He wondered if she had some of the same thoughts.

"Why don't the characters in your books ever have oral sex?"

He laughed. Of all the burning questions he imagined she might have, that wasn't one of them. He wasn't even sure how to answer.

But she was obviously interested in this topic because she layered on another question. "Didn't the people back in the Old West do that stuff?"

"I haven't given it much thought, but I'll bet they did. Couples have been enjoying oral sex throughout history, so the Old West wouldn't have been that different."

"How about sex with the woman astride?"

This was the strangest conversation. "I'm sure they

did that, too. Ladies of the night were popular back in those days, and the more innovative ones probably made the most money."

"But nice girls stuck with the missionary position, I suppose."

He rolled to his side and gazed at her. "I don't know that, either. People are endlessly inventive in the bedroom. Who knows what they did when the candles were snuffed?"

She turned to face him and her green eyes sparkled. "Do you suppose their men took them from behind once in a while?"

"I wouldn't doubt it. For one thing, if a woman's pregnant, especially if she's pretty far along, I've heard that's the most comfortable way to have sex."

"I hadn't thought of that. It would be. And just because a woman has a big belly doesn't mean she doesn't want an orgasm now and then. Or that he doesn't want to enjoy the pleasures of his lovely wife."

He was transfixed by the image of making love to her when she was pregnant with his child. How dumb was that? Their relationship might not survive past this week, let alone blossom into a permanent commitment that resulted in her being pregnant with his kid.

Even so, the image of taking her to bed when she was in that special condition wouldn't leave him. He felt a tenderness that had absolutely no basis in fact. For one thing, she might not even *want* children, let alone children who carried his genetic code.

Finally he asked the obvious question. "Why are you so interested in the sex lives of people in the nineteenth century?"

"Because I read your books."

"I know you do." That's what had landed them in this briar patch, or more accurately, in this bed of roses. He now owed a huge, impossible-to-calculate debt to his publisher for causing him to meet Keri. Fortunately his publishing house would never know the role it played, so he wouldn't have to make any kind of grand gesture.

"I'm only one reader, and I know you must have thousands."

"I do, now. I didn't in the beginning, but business is picking up."

She smiled. "It should. You're a terrific writer."

"Thanks." He was a little embarrassed to be having this discussion while he was naked with a woman he'd recently... Oh, yes, he certainly had. And he'd loved every single thrust into her warm body, every taste of her juices on his tongue, every whimper she'd uttered when he'd touched her in those secret, fragrant places. He'd loved the way her pupils dilated when she was ready to come. He loved the way she arched into his caress, and how she quivered when he—

"I wish you'd put more hot sex in your books," she said.

He blinked, disoriented. "What?"

"You have a really sexy style—strong, masculine, commanding. I wanted to see that masterful behavior in the bedroom. I wanted the scenes to crackle, with the cowboy hero taking charge and stripping her naked, or maybe the heroine pushing him back on that coverlet and straddling him. I wanted you to make me squirm in my bed while I was reading those pages, but...you pulled your punches."

He stared at her. "The stories aren't about sex."

"Everything's about sex."

He started to contradict her, but then he realized she was right. Sampson and Delilah. Anthony and Cleopatra. Napoleon and Josephine. From the famous lovers of the past to current scandals in the headlines, sex changed lives and altered the course of history.

"I wondered if maybe Jim Ford wasn't very creative in bed," she continued, "so those scenes would necessarily be boring. But you're not boring in bed, Michael."

"That's something, at least." He faced another decision—whether to make excuses or tell her the truth. He opted for the truth. "I didn't know if I could write good sex scenes, so I skimmed over them."

She held his gaze. "You can write good sex scenes. I know that you can after spending two glorious nights in your bed. You only have to give yourself permission to let that side of you come out in the writing. And after all, it's only Jim Ford doing it. Nobody knows Jim Ford, really."

"You do."

"And I'll never tell."

He wasn't worried in the least that she would tell. No, the real worry was whether or not he was capable of writing a sex scene that conveyed the intensity he'd experienced with her. If he failed, he'd know it from her expression.

He'd suffered through bad reviews before, but always once removed, something he saw in print or online. Because he didn't interact much with readers for fear they'd discover his identity, he'd seldom had someone criticize him to his face.

Not that Keri would attack. She would be kind, regardless of whether she liked what he'd written. But if he hadn't met her expectations, he'd know it. That could be rough.

Still, she'd issued a challenge no writer worth his salt could ignore. They talked a little more about the subject, but he didn't agree or disagree that he should beef up those scenes. Privately, he knew he was going to give it a shot and then decide if he'd show her what he'd done.

He waited until she finally drifted off to sleep. Then he slipped out of bed and pulled his laptop from its case. If he planned to do this thing, he'd best do it now, when his nostrils were filled with the scent of her and his body throbbed with remembered pleasure. Lying naked in his bed, she'd provide all the inspiration any man should need. God help him, he wanted to please her in this, too.

12

KERI WOKE TO the peppy phone melody she used as an alarm. It didn't take her long to remember where she was. Michael's big body spooned hers, and his arm was tucked around her waist. When she tried to reach her phone the weight of his arm held her back.

She tried to ease away, in case he was still sleeping. He pulled her close. Obviously *not* sleeping. "Let me go, Michael."

"I don't want to."

"I'll bet you don't." She rubbed her fanny against his hard penis. "But we don't have time for that."

"Sure we do. You proved that you can get dressed in twenty minutes." His hand moved down her belly headed for an obvious destination.

Laughing, she grabbed his hand and stopped its downward movement. "And that's all the time I gave myself when I set the alarm. Sorry, Romeo."

"Damn."

She brought his hand up to her mouth and kissed it. "I can change that tomorrow morning and give us a little more time."

"I guess you'd better. I expect to be waking up this way tomorrow, too." He sighed and flopped onto his back.

"How much extra time will you need?" Moving to the edge of the bed, she grabbed the phone and shut off the alarm.

"An hour."

She rolled to face him. "An *hour?* You want to wake up an hour early so we can have sex?"

He grinned at her, his smile very white against his beard-darkened face. "You're right. That's not enough. Make it two hours."

"You're insane." Smiling, she climbed out of bed and tossed the sheet over the lower half of his body.

He surveyed the result. "Oh, look, a circus tent. It's the Greatest Show on—"

"Sorry, but this part of the circus is leaving town." She started toward the door.

"If you could see yourself, you'd understand why I'm in this condition."

"I don't know what you mean." She pivoted and glanced down. "It's just plain old me."

"There's nothing plain about you." He propped his hands behind his head. "You're all pink, tousled and sleepy-eyed. Take a look in the mirror when you get a chance. You're the most ready-for-sex woman I've ever seen in my life."

She rolled her eyes. "Nice try, but I'm still leaving. Have a good day." She headed for the door again.

"Thanks. You, too. Oh, and Keri?"

"What?" She turned back to him with a show of impatience. She thought he was adorable with his stalling routine, but she couldn't let him know that or he'd drag her back to bed.

"I wonder if…well, if you have time, if you'd take a look at the sex scene I wrote last night. I labeled the file *Sex Scene* so it would be easy for you to find on my laptop."

She stared at him as two things registered. He'd been writing while she slept, and he valued her opinion. He valued it so much, in fact, that he'd immediately attempted to correct the flaw she'd pointed out in his books.

Praising her sex appeal was one thing. Men complimented women on that all the time. But Michael had listened to her suggestion about his work and had put his ego aside to act on that suggestion. That took a special kind of guy.

"You might not have time, though," he said. "It's okay if you don't."

"I'll make time." She walked over to the bed and picked up a condom from the nightstand. "I'd be honored to read your scene." She handed him the condom.

"What's this for? I thought you were leaving?"

"I'll dress a little faster today. I hear the circus is in town." And she climbed back into bed.

"STAY WITH HIM! Stay with him!" Jack shouted encouragement as Michael focused on the constantly shifting motion of Finicky, one of Gabe Chance's prime cutting horses. Michael had tried to talk Jack out of using this valuable horse for a beginner, but Jack had insisted that either the horse or the rider had to know what he was doing or they'd have chaos.

Finicky, a chocolate-and-white Paint, was obviously the knowledgeable one in this pairing. Jack had released four steers into the corral, and Finicky was charged with singling out one of them and herding it into a pen. Michael was simply along for the ride, but if he didn't concentrate he'd land on his butt in the dirt. That had happened once already, and he didn't want it happening again.

"That's it," Jack said. "Now you're feeling it. See if you can let go of the horn and stay on. Holding on to the horn will not impress the ladies."

Finicky swerved with the precision of a Formula One racer, and Michael almost didn't make the turn with him. "I'm not ready for that, Jack."

"Sure you are. Stop thinking and let yourself feel the motion of the horse. He'll telegraph his moves if you're paying attention. Remember the analogy we talked about yesterday."

Michael knew exactly what analogy Jack was referring to, and fortunately he hadn't shouted it out where anyone passing by could hear. But Keri was a dangerous topic for Michael right now. If he thought of her, he pictured her reading what he'd written last night, and he broke out in a cold sweat.

He wanted to master this cutting horse business, though, so he let go of the horn and tried to anticipate Finicky's next move. He failed to do that. Next thing he knew, he'd slid neatly out of the saddle and landed with a thud in the middle of the dusty corral.

Jack hopped the fence and came over to collect the horse and hold out a hand to Michael. "What's the problem, buddy? You were doing great yesterday. Did something go wrong upstairs?"

"Nope." Michael picked up his hat and slapped it against his jeans to knock off some of the dust. "All's well."

"You're not thinking about that, though, are you?"

"I might've made a mistake."

Jack frowned. "I hope you're not talking about doing it bareback, because that's not acceptable."

"For God's sake, Jack. I wouldn't take that kind of risk. Give me some credit."

"Well, when you used the word *mistake,* my mind naturally went to that kind of mistake. What did you do, then?"

Michael took a deep breath. "I asked her to read a scene out of my current manuscript."

"You did?" Jack beamed at him as if Michael were a star pupil. "That's *great.* She will totally love that you asked her to do that. What a way to make points. Well done."

"Yeah, but…" Michael settled his hat on his head. "What if she doesn't like it?"

"Why wouldn't she? Is it too bloody? Did you have some bad guys hack up a sweet old grandma or something heinous like that?"

Michael laughed. "I don't write about sweet old grandmas getting hacked to bits. You should know that."

"You haven't so far, but there's always a first time. If you were dumb enough to let her read something like that, no wonder you're falling off Finicky, here." He reached over and stroked the horse's nose.

"It was a sex scene."

"Oh, well, then. You're in high cotton, my friend. She'll think she inspired you."

"She did."

"Then you can't lose. She'll feel a part of your creative process and get turned on in the bargain. I don't know what you're worried about. That was a brilliant move. If I'd have thought of it, I would have told you to do exactly that."

Michael scratched Finicky's neck. "She said my sex scenes weren't hot enough."

"Really?" Jack cocked his head as if mentally reviewing sex scenes by Jim Ford. "I thought they were fine, but I don't read your books for that. I like the gunfights."

"She likes the sex."

"That's natural, and there's nothing wrong with making them hotter, especially for your female readers. You might increase your audience that way. You should listen to Keri."

"I did, but now I'm worried that she won't like what I wrote."

Jack clapped him on the shoulder. "I'm sure you wrote that scene just fine. I guarantee she's already read it, so you can't change the situation now. What's done is done."

Michael nodded. "You have a point."

"And this afternoon you want to impress her with your riding abilities, so you need to get back on that horse and think about what you actually did in bed last night, not how you wrote about it later on."

Michael tugged his hat brim down. "That's good advice, Jack. Let's try this again." He swung into the saddle.

"Now you're talking like a cowboy." He gave Finicky a whack on his flank, and the horse went back to work cutting cattle.

Focusing on the sensation of moving effortlessly toward a climax with Keri, Michael began to sense the rhythm of the horse. He couldn't carry that analogy too far. Keri was not a horse and he was certainly not her rider. But the cooperative effort had some similarities.

Writing was a mental exercise, and he'd been thinking again. Once he settled back into his physical body, he could let go of the horn and shift his weight with Finicky's abrupt changes in direction. After a while, it felt like dancing, except he was in the position of follower. That was new, but he'd get used to it.

And sometime this afternoon, he'd put on a show for Keri. Jack had recommended it, and the more Michael hung out with Jack the more he saw the wisdom of following Jack's recommendations. The guy knew about horses and women. Michael was more than willing to learn more about both subjects.

As the lunch hour approached, Keri struggled with logistics. She wanted time alone with Michael, both to tell him how great his scene had been and to satisfy her craving for at least one kiss. Reading that scene had made her want him with a desperation that was alarming.

After much thought, she could see no solution other than taking Mary Lou into her confidence. They'd made a cowboy favorite—ribs, baked beans and coleslaw. The hands would file in any minute, and Keri needed an ally.

She checked the simmering beans. They smelled

wonderful, as always. Lately Keri's senses had been more alert than ever in her life. Food smelled amazing and tasted even better. She paid more attention to the birds singing outside the kitchen window. Her skin was more sensitive to touch, and wherever she looked she saw beauty.

Mary Lou pulled the first pan of ribs out of the commercial oven. "Bring me the platters, Keri. It's time to get these ready to serve."

"You bet." Keri took the platters out of a bottom cupboard and helped Mary Lou load them. "I have a big favor to ask."

"Sure, honey. Name it."

Steam from the ribs surrounded them. The kitchen was hot, and tendrils of hair had escaped Keri's ponytail to curl damply at her neck. Ordinarily she'd be wishing for a cool breeze, but today the fiery need for Michael that burned within her made the external temperature unimportant.

"I need a moment alone with Michael."

Mary Lou chuckled. "I had a feeling he'd be what the favor was about." She used tongs to load another platter. "How can I help?"

"When the hands start coming in, I'll head out into the backyard. If you could tell Michael to come out and find me there, I'd be very grateful. We won't be long. I won't leave you in the lurch."

"You won't." Mary Lou took the last pan of ribs out of the oven. "I'll get Watkins to help me put out the food. That man will do anything I ask him."

Keri moved the filled platter and replaced it with an empty one. "Really? How did you manage that?"

"It's very simple." Mary Lou leaned close to murmur her secret. "Blow jobs."

Keri grinned. "You go, Mary Lou."

"Don't tell him I said so."

"I wouldn't dream of it." Keri couldn't imagine having that conversation with the stocky cowhand under any circumstances, but it was extremely cute that Mary Lou thought she might. "Thanks so much for letting me duck out for a minute."

"I'm glad to help. I like seeing two young people in love."

"Oh, it's not love." The minute she said that, the statement felt false. But she didn't have time to mentally debate the issue.

"In lust, then. One can look a lot like the other."

"Yes, it can." Keri didn't want to get confused about that.

"I hear them coming in. Go on out back, and I'll send Michael to find you when I see him."

"Thanks, Mary Lou." Keri squeezed her arm. "You're the best."

Mary Lou winked at her. "That's what Watkins says, too."

Keri walked through a side door and out onto a little deck where Mary Lou often took her morning coffee break. A set of steps led down to the yard, where Mary Lou's small garden was protected from critters by a chicken-wire fence and bird netting. Keri knew she would miss a great deal about the Last Chance when she ended her employment here, but leaving Mary Lou might be the hardest part of all.

Her thoughts about her future were a jumbled mess.

She wanted to move permanently to Jackson Hole, but she hadn't decided where to look for a job. The city of Jackson was the logical place to start if she wanted a PR job, but she'd rather stay in a more rural area like this one.

Oh, well. Her decision to stay was brand-new, and it wasn't like she was leaving tomorrow. She'd figure it out. But her feelings for Michael complicated things. By remaining here, she'd put a lot of miles between them. If she returned to her old life, they could see each other on weekends.

Much as she now wanted that, she couldn't face living the way she had before, not even for the prospect of being closer to Michael. So while she'd worked today, she'd given more thought to what kind of job she could get here that would suit her training. One possibility would be perfect. But she didn't know if Bethany Grace needed a personal assistant.

The self-help author, who was currently honeymooning with her new husband, Nash Bledsoe, would eventually return and set up housekeeping with Nash on the Triple G, a small ranch next door to the Last Chance. In addition to her writing career, Bethany planned to host retreats for burned-out CEOs.

Nash would give riding lessons and lead trail rides for those who wanted that experience, and Bethany would conduct mini-seminars on living a balanced life. Keri could manage Bethany's schedule and provide some PR for the retreat venture. But until Bethany and Nash came home, she couldn't find out if her idea was viable or not. Bethany might already have someone in mind for that job. Keri decided to ask Jack and see what he knew.

The back door opened and she turned as Michael walked out. He looked more like a broad-shouldered, lean-hipped cowboy every day. Even the tilt of his Stetson seemed more authentic.

He smiled, crossed the deck in two strides and bounded down the steps.

She hurried over to meet him. Wasting no time, she threw her arms around his neck and kissed him so enthusiastically he lost his hat. He didn't seem to care. With a moan, he pulled her close and thrust his tongue into her mouth.

She couldn't seem to get close enough. Burrowing against him, she felt the rapid beat of his heart and the ridge of his cock. His breathing roughened and he cupped her bottom to press her tighter against his fly.

Erotic visions flashed through her mind. Maybe, in the shadow of the trees, they could...no. She'd promised Mary Lou she wouldn't be out here long.

I like to see young people in love.

Mary Lou's words came back to her. But this was lust. This deep craving was about sex. Maybe, given enough time together, they'd—

Michael lifted his mouth a fraction but held her firmly in place. His breath was warm on her kiss-moistened lips. "Let's skip lunch."

"I can't."

He groaned. "Damn. Guess I should be grateful for what I have, huh? One more kiss. Then we'll go in and—"

"Wait." She pressed her finger against his mouth. "I need to say something, first. Your scene is wonderful."

He drew back to look into her eyes. "It is?"

She nodded. "Women readers are going to love it. *I* loved it. Reading it made me hot."

The corners of his mouth tilted up. "I seduced you with a few paragraphs of my deathless prose?"

"Yeah, you sure did."

"If this is your response, I'll cancel my riding lessons and head back to the computer. Jack claims you'll be turned on by watching me penning steers on Finicky this afternoon, but obviously he doesn't know what he's talking about."

"You want me to watch you ride?"

"Not anymore. Writing a sex scene is a hell of a lot easier for me than trying to stay in the saddle of a cutting horse." He nudged her gently with his hips. "And apparently the writing works just fine."

"But I want to watch you ride."

"No, you don't. If I look like a fool, then I'll lose all the ground I gained with that sex scene. Instead of watching me ride, go read that file again."

He sure could make her smile. She noticed that his eyes always seemed more blue than gray when he was teasing her. The longer she held his gaze the more she wanted to stay right here, tucked against his warm body. She plain liked being with him.

He took a deep breath. "You need to get back inside."

"We both do. You have to eat lunch so you'll be fueled up for your cutting horse demonstration."

"Let's forget about that. It was all Jack's idea, not mine."

"I want to watch. Tell me what time."

"He mentioned four o'clock, but—"

"I'll be there."

"I'd rather have you in my room, reading that scene. I look much better on paper."

"You look good no matter what you're doing."

His eyebrows lifted. "Thanks. You, too. We seem to have a mutual admiration society going."

"Seems like it."

He looked into her eyes for a long moment, and when he spoke, his voice had lost every trace of teasing. "Maybe we should talk about that."

She'd meant to lead up to this subject, not drop it like a bombshell, but instead she blurted it out with no finesse whatsoever. "I've been meaning to tell you. I'm moving here. Permanently."

Shock registered in his expression. He clearly hadn't been expecting that. "Oh."

"I thought you should know."

"Yeah. Yeah, that is good to know." The warm light had left his eyes. "Well, let's get back, so we don't cause any problems." He released her and picked up his hat from the grass.

"Michael, what we've shared has been...*is* important to me."

"I know." His wry smile tore at her heart. "For me, too. But life goes on, doesn't it?"

13

MICHAEL THOUGHT HE'D done a pretty good job of acting normal at lunch, but Jack had spent enough time with him to figure out something wasn't right. He started asking questions as they walked down to the barn after the meal was over.

"You had a chance to talk to Keri before lunch, right?"

"Yeah."

"Did you ask her to come down around four and watch the team penning?"

"I told her about it." Michael kept walking. He felt like a first-class fool for thinking he and Keri were building a relationship that had potential. When she'd announced she was leaving her job here, he'd assumed she'd go home to Baltimore where she'd be a short train ride away. Apparently she'd changed her plans.

"Is she coming or not?"

"I don't know. Probably."

"You're mighty sparse with the info, buddy. What's up?"

Michael glanced at him. Keri had said she was moving here permanently, but she hadn't said whether she planned to keep working as a housekeeper at the Last Chance. Even if she had said that, he wasn't the person to tell Jack about it. "Just a little misunderstanding, that's all."

"She didn't like your sex scene?"

"Oh, no. She loved it. You were right about that. She appreciated being asked to read it and as a result of reading it, she was turned on."

"Excellent! So what's the problem? When Mary Lou sent you out to find Keri you were riding high. Happy didn't even begin to describe the expression on your face. Now you look as if you just finished watching *Old Yeller.*"

"Sorry."

"Me, too. Finicky likes you a lot better when you're cheerful."

That made him chuckle, in spite of himself. "I wouldn't want to get on the bad side of Finicky, that's for damned sure."

"I didn't think so. No matter what sort of misunderstanding took place out behind the house, you want Finicky to be in a good mood, so put on your happy face, little buckaroo."

Michael sighed. "Jack, did anybody ever tell you that you're a royal pain in the ass?"

"Once or twice."

"Well, I'm telling you again."

"Duly noted." Jack clapped him on the shoulder. "I have an idea. Before we go back out to the corral, let's muck us out a few stalls. You will be amazed at how that improves a fellow's disposition. I've been remiss in not introducing you to that particular type of therapy."

"Is that what you call it? Therapy?"

"I do, and I'm not the only one. You ask any cowboy how he works through his problems, and he'll give you one of four answers. He rides like hell, gets drunk, picks a fight or shovels shit. Since we're not going to run any of our horses in the middle of a hot day, and I'm not prepared to get you plastered or fight with you, that leaves us with mucking out stalls."

Michael considered that option. It sounded pretty good, actually. Something sweaty and mindless. "How do you know there are stalls to be mucked out? Maybe the other guys have taken care of it already."

"My friend, when you own as many horses as we do, there will *always* be mucking to be done. Horses eat an uncommon amount of food and horses poop an uncommon amount of shit. The opportunity for that type of therapy never ends."

"Then lead me to it."

AROUND THREE-FORTY-FIVE, Keri walked down to the barn and the corrals. She felt terrible about the abrupt way she'd informed Michael about her recent decision to stay in Wyoming. When he implied that they needed to discuss their future, she could have agreed with him and then waited until they had more time together before hitting him with her revised plans.

Of course, if she'd told him sooner, instead of reveling in great sex and pushing that other issue aside, he'd never have made that comment in the first place. She wondered how much would have changed between them if she'd laid out her future plans earlier, as she'd intended to.

Michael probably would have wanted to continue having sex. Guys seldom turned down that option if they were attracted to the woman in question. But he might not have been so open with her, and he might not have asked her to read the sex scene. Maybe he wouldn't have written it in the first place.

In her heart of hearts, she believed he'd created that scene for her, as a present. She'd asked for something, and he'd decided to grant her request. If that hadn't been his motivation, why show it to her? It definitely had been offered in the spirit of a gift.

Her heart ached when she remembered how his eyes had dulled when he'd heard her news. She didn't think he'd reached the stage of wanting a commitment, but no doubt he'd hoped they could continue what was obviously working out well for both of them. He might have had a hazy idea that it could develop into something serious eventually.

Her timing had been terrible, just terrible. First she'd kissed him as if she couldn't imagine life without him, and then, when he'd naturally followed up on that enthusiasm with a rational statement about what might come next, she'd shot him down. Talk about mixed messages.

She would apologize once she had a chance, but that wouldn't fix anything. The damage had been done, and she'd been the one responsible. If he wanted to end their relationship now and save himself potential heartache, she wouldn't blame him.

All things considered, she expected Michael to be in a somber mood when he put on this demonstration, assuming he put it on at all. Instead, he was grinning as he stood in the middle of the corral with Jack and Jack's younger brother, Gabe. Gabe had inherited his mother Sarah's fair coloring and was currently sporting a mustache.

Each of the men held the reins of his horse, and they seemed to be having a jolly time hanging out together. From the way they were laughing, Keri thought they were trading insults or bawdy jokes as they waited for the steers to be brought in.

Several other cowboys lined the corral railing, along with Emmett Sterling and his daughter, Emily. Putting a foot on the bottom rail, Keri pulled herself up to lean on the top rail beside Emily. She and Emily had liked each other from the first day Keri had arrived at the ranch.

Emily's blond hair was tucked up under her hat and she was chewing on a piece of straw. Keri got a kick out of that. Emmett had the same habit, and his daughter was mirroring him, either consciously or unconsciously.

Emily took the piece of straw from her mouth and glanced over at Keri. "Hey there, girlfriend. Gonna watch the greenhorn do his stuff?"

"I thought I would." She looked around for Emily's husband, who ran the stud program for the ranch. "Where's Clay?"

"He had to straighten out a shipping problem and he's stuck inside on the phone. Somehow a canister of sperm arrived unfrozen and spoiled. Clay expects the shipping company to pay for it, but they're giving him a song and dance."

Keri smiled. "They've picked the wrong guy to mess with."

"Yes, indeedy. I know from personal experience that he's very persistent." Emily's blue eyes shone with pride. She was obviously crazy about Clay Whitaker.

"The Last Chance is lucky to have him."

"Yep. And so am I." Emily gestured toward the corral. "I hear Michael's really coming along with this riding gig."

"I hope so. He wants to learn."

Emily hesitated. "This is clearly none of my business, but word around the ranch is that you like him a lot."

"I do."

"Good." Emily looked happy with the answer. "I can see you two together."

"Uh...we're not exactly *together*." And wouldn't ever be.

"Okay, didn't mean to imply anything. Whatever the deal is, you'd make a cute couple. Your accents are almost the same."

Keri latched on to that remark with gratitude. She blinked innocently. "What accent?"

"Yeah, right. Don't get me started. You have the accent. We don't. End of story."

"Easterners set the standard." She smiled at Emily. "Everything else is a variation." It was a running joke between them, and Keri welcomed the chance to kid around, even about something as silly as accents.

"Not a variation. An improvement." Emily winked and returned her attention to the corral. "Here come the critters."

Six white-faced Herefords, the small herd the ranch kept for training purposes, trotted into the corral. The men mounted up. Michael swung into the saddle like a pro.

Keri didn't recognize all the Last Chance horses, but she knew the one Michael was riding. The chocolate-and-white gelding was featured in many framed pictures sitting in the ranch's trophy cabinet, a cabinet Keri was in charge of dusting.

She turned to Emily. "Gabe's letting Michael ride Finicky?"

Emily nodded. "He and Jack wanted Michael to learn on a well-trained horse, and Finicky's the best. Michael looks good on him."

"Yes, he does." Keri realized she'd said that with a little too much enthusiasm when Emily grinned at her. "They all look good," she added quickly. "Are Jack and Bandit going to participate?" Everyone on the ranch knew Bandit, the most valuable stud on the ranch, had been laid up recently.

"No, Bandit's not up to it yet, although I'm sure he's bored silly. Jack probably wants to give him a little outing without doing anything strenuous first. Jack can keep an eye on things while Gabe and Michael work the cattle. I love watching Jack on Bandit, though. He and that horse are a unit. As for Gabe, he can ride any horse and make it look like a champion."

"Who's he up on?"

"That's Rorschach. It's tough to tell them apart if you're not down here every day like I am. It's especially hard when they're both black-and-white, like Rorschach and Bandit. Rorschach doesn't have the eye patches. Or the attitude."

"I see what you mean about Bandit's attitude." Keri's

gaze followed the horse as he pranced around the corral, neck arched and tail flying like a flag. He didn't seem to be favoring his leg at all. "I think Jack encourages him."

Emily laughed. "You think?"

But impressive as Jack and Bandit looked circling the corral, and as obviously accomplished as Gabe was on his horse, Keri couldn't take her eyes off Michael. Seeing him now, she couldn't believe he was a novice. As he sat easily in the saddle, his back straight and his hands loose on the reins, he looked every inch a cowboy.

She turned to Emily. "I'm excited to see this demonstration. I've never watched team penning, before."

"You're in for a treat. Gabe's a super rider, and he'll get the most out of Rorschach. Finicky's a great horse, and he'll get the most out of Michael. The pairing is brilliant, really. Michael should have a lot of fun if he can stay on."

"He might not?" Keri's stomach churned.

"He probably will. But I'll bet that's why Jack's there, in case things get crazy and Michael needs a quick pickup."

Keri hadn't even considered that Michael might get dumped in the dirt, caught in a whirlpool of churning animals and sharp hooves. Her heart beat faster as her anxiety level rose.

"Don't look so scared. He'll be fine."

"He'd better be," she muttered. If Jack had put Michael in danger just so they could all show off, she would never forgive him.

As the penning operation began, she clenched her jaw and tightened her grip on the rail. At one point she felt a little dizzy and realized she was also holding her breath. And praying. This wasn't fun at all.

Michael, however, seemed to be having a blast. He was concentrating hard, but that didn't stop the grin from popping out whenever he and Finicky executed a tricky maneuver. As dust flew and cowboys whooped, the two men and their horses cut a steer from the milling herd and worked it neatly into the pen.

They repeated the feat again with no mishaps, and Keri began to relax. But the third steer wasn't so cooperative. Finicky was determined and turned a corner with such blinding speed that Michael lost a stirrup and started to slide.

Keri gasped and clutched Emily's arm.

Jack shouted something to Michael, who grabbed the saddle horn and righted himself. Finicky seemed to take no notice of Michael's behavior. He focused on the steer and pivoted like a dancer as he blocked the animal's attempt to escape. Gabe worked the steer's other side, and Michael eventually regained his stirrup and became part of the action again. They penned the steer.

"There, see?" Emily glanced at Keri. "He stayed on."

"Just barely." She blew out a breath and let go of Emily's arm. "Sorry if I left a bruise."

"Nah, I'm tough."

Jack called for a break and rode over to talk with Michael and Gabe. Keri was reminded of a coach coming out on the baseball field to consult with his players. Both Gabe and Michael nodded. Then they all laughed.

That laughter did more to sooth Keri's jangled nerves than anything else. "I guess everything's okay if they can laugh about it."

Emily glanced at her. "I'll bet you've never been in love with a cowboy before, have you?"

"I'm not..." She didn't finish the sentence because Emily gave her a look that said she wasn't buying any denial on Keri's part. For emphasis, Emily held up her arm, with little pink spots where Keri had grabbed her.

Keri sighed. "No, I've never been in love with a cowboy before." She was beginning to wonder if she'd ever been in love before, period. No man in recent memory had affected her with this bone-deep yearning. Or this paralyzing fear for his safety.

"The thing is, they're modern-day knights. That means they take physical risks to challenge themselves, and you have to be okay with that. Sometimes they get banged up, and you have to be okay with that, too, because they don't take well to being fussed over."

"I already know that about Michael." She remembered Michael's stubborn insistence that he was fine, when she knew he had to be in pain. "But he's not really a cowboy yet."

"Oh, I think he is." Emily turned back to the corral where Gabe and Michael prepared to pen another steer.

"How can you tell?"

"He didn't quit after the humiliation of having to reach for the horn."

"What was humiliating about that?"

Emily looked at her. "Grabbing the saddle horn is not macho. I suspect he was willing to go down rather than hold on until Jack yelled at him not to be stupid. So now he wants to prove he can finish the event without doing that again." She smiled. "That's typical cowboy thinking."

Keri groaned. "I don't know if I can watch the rest of this. If he falls, then he could get trampled."

"Jack and Gabe are there to keep that from happening."

"But you just said cowboys sometimes get banged up." The image of Michael lying on the ground, bloody and unconscious, made her sick to her stomach.

"They do get banged up. And I won't kid you. He's not perfectly safe in there. I hope you stay, though. If he's like most cowboys, he's doing this for you."

14

MICHAEL WOULD BE damned if he'd grab the saddle horn again, despite what Jack had said at the break. In fact, Jack had mentioned several things. He'd alluded to Michael's inability to write any more bestsellers if a horse or a cow stepped on his fingers. He'd added that choosing image over safety was ridiculous and that impressing a woman wasn't worth getting stomped on by critters.

Jack was probably right about all of that. Maybe if Keri hadn't said she was staying in Wyoming, which essentially meant she wouldn't be seeing much of him in the future, he might not have felt so hell-bent on showing off. But if he was going to become only a memory, he wanted to be a good one.

Of course, he wouldn't be such a good memory if he got himself trampled right in front of her. So he couldn't let that happen. That meant he had to stop thinking and simply feel the motion of the horse beneath him. As Jack had said, it was a lot like having sex with a woman.

All afternoon he'd considered how Keri's announcement would affect their sexual relationship for the rest of this week. By choosing not to live in Baltimore she'd changed everything. He couldn't blame her for that choice. He certainly didn't want her to be miserable in Baltimore just so they could see if they were meant to be together.

But now, instead of anticipating a continuation of their affair, he would leave knowing it was over. Tomorrow the wedding guests would arrive, and he and Keri wouldn't be alone upstairs. That didn't completely cut out the possibility of sex, but…it wouldn't be the same.

It wasn't the same, anyway. He might be able to act as if nothing had changed when they were in bed together, but everything had. He'd foolishly started to fall for her, but he was finished with that nonsense.

As he waited for Gabe's signal to start working the cattle again, he glanced across the corral at Keri. Pain sliced through his heart, and he cursed softly. He hadn't *started* to fall for her. He'd fallen, and hard. He couldn't let her see that.

If he called a halt to their affair, that protective move would telegraph his feelings. He might as well write it out in glowing neon. As he thought of that, he knew how tonight would go.

Tonight would be all about physical gratification, and he would be fine with that. She'd be fine with it, too. He'd make sure she was so blissed out by multiple orgasms that she never noticed his emotions weren't in play. Yep, if he was going to be a memory, she'd need a fan and a bucket of ice whenever she thought of him. Guaranteed.

That decision brought a focus he'd lacked before. When Gabe nodded, Michael was ready to go. No more overthinking his actions. He'd let his body do its thing and simply roll with it.

When it came to the team penning, Michael was stunned by the spectacular results. He didn't miss a single cue Finicky gave him. Neither did he kid himself that he was a pro who could ride any cutting horse in the world. Finicky's expertise was a big part of the smooth operation. But at least he wasn't a hindrance this time.

When it was all over, he got plenty of compliments from the cowhands lining the rail. Jack and Gabe both rode over to shake his hand. When he happened to look at Keri, she gave him a thumbs up and a big smile. He might be the only one who noticed that her smile trembled a little bit.

The thought crossed his mind that she might be battling some feelings for him, too. Maybe ending their affair wouldn't be a walk in the park for her, either. In that case, maybe he should ask her what she wanted, rather than assuming they'd head upstairs tonight for their last hurrah.

Hell, he was back to overthinking his decisions. If she didn't want to have sex with him tonight, she would say so. She'd never been particularly shy with him.

He rode Finicky through the corral gate on his way to the hitching post in front of the barn. Clay Whitaker had arrived, and Keri stood talking with him and Emily. As Michael rode past them, Keri glanced up and he touched the brim of his hat the way he'd seen Jack and the other cowboys do when they met a woman.

She smiled again, and this time there was no doubt. It was the saddest smile he'd ever seen in his life. She *was* miserable, and he couldn't ignore that and pretend he didn't see her distress. He wasn't built that way.

But now wasn't the time to deal with it. He'd ridden Finicky hard, and the horse deserved a good rubdown and a handful of oats. Gabe and Jack had already tied their horses to the hitching post.

"Great job," Jack said as Michael rode up.

Michael laughed. "Are you talking to me or the horse?"

"The horse, but you weren't so bad, yourself." He pulled his saddle and blanket off and started into the barn.

"Thanks!" Michael called after him.

Gabe lifted his saddle and blanket off Rorschach. "You hit your stride after we took that break."

"Yeah." Michael dismounted and tied Finicky to the rail. "I finally got in sync with this amazing horse. I'm sure he could do the job without me, though."

"He could, but he wouldn't. He's trained to do this with a rider on board. He's not a sheepdog."

Michael unbuckled the cinch. "Well, I'm honored that I got to be that rider, Gabe. Thanks for letting me pretend to be the real deal for an afternoon."

"Hey, you're well on your way to becoming the real deal. You've got the right stuff. Are you sure you don't want to stick around a little longer?"

"Unfortunately, I can't." He glanced at Gabe. "Wish I could, but I have to get back." He had a meeting with his agent and his editor on Tuesday to discuss the details of his next contract, which should include a sizable bump in his advance money. On Wednesday he'd be on a plane to California, where the video would be made.

"Could you schedule another week or two out here before the snow flies? I hate to see you go months without riding when you're so close to really getting it."

"I'll think about that." He wished he could, but with his book sales increasing, his publisher had pushed up the publication date for his next release. That meant some long hours at the keyboard. "Thanks for the invite. And the confidence in me."

"You bet." Gabe left for the barn.

Michael followed soon after, and he met Jack coming out with a bucket full of grooming supplies. He lowered his voice. "Don't look now, but Keri's headed this way."

"Oh?" Michael hoped he looked unaffected by that news.

"If you want to take your time putting your saddle away, I could send her in there so you two can have a more private discussion."

"I can talk to her out here."

"I dunno. She looks like a woman who would like to have a word, and that usually requires privacy."

"Okay." Belatedly, Michael realized they should talk and establish how things were going to be between them tonight. Maybe she would be the one to call it off. God, he hoped not. He wasn't ready to let her go quite yet.

He continued into the cool shadows of the barn and put his saddle and blanket away. Some shape he was in for a close encounter with a woman. He and Jack had worked up a sweat shoveling manure earlier that afternoon.

The therapy had worked like a charm, too. Michael had relaxed into the rhythm of a working ranch, and his stress had melted away, until the moment he'd looked over at the corral fence and spotted Keri. Then he'd tightened up again.

Needing to move, he walked down the wooden aisle between the stalls. He'd let this woman get to him, and that was entirely his fault. He'd wanted her from day one, and once the barriers were gone he'd been only too eager to enjoy the charms of Keri Fitzpatrick.

That wouldn't have been a mistake if he'd thought of it as a brief affair. But he hadn't done that. When he'd seen the possibility for more, he'd let his imagination have at it.

Shaking his head, he admitted that he'd pictured a romantic reunion at Penn Station. Somehow he'd always imagined her coming to New York, instead of him traveling to Baltimore. In his mind, they'd walked through Central Park, wandered the halls of the Metropolitan Museum, held hands during a Broadway play and eaten pasta at his favorite little place on Restaurant Row.

They'd also made love in his apartment—in the bedroom, in the living room and even in the kitchen. Oh, yeah, he'd mentally placed Keri firmly in his life and in his bed. Only problem was, she had no intention of going there.

"Michael?" She stood in the doorway of the barn, a shadow outlined in golden light. She didn't seem quite real, and he felt her loss as if she'd already disappeared from his life.

"I'm here." He walked toward her, the sound of his boots on the floorboards echoing in the stillness.

"Jack said I should come and find you." She stepped into the barn, and the soft glow from the lights set at floor level along the aisle made her look more ethereal than ever.

He had an overwhelming urge to hold her and convince himself she wasn't some figment of his overactive imagination. Closing the distance between them, he gathered her close. "I've missed you."

She didn't ask what he meant by that strange comment. They'd only been apart a few hours. But they'd been separated by a gulf wider than hours. She seemed to understand that as she wrapped her arms around his waist and held on tight. "I've missed you, too."

His plan to stay emotionally distant crumbled. Instead, he told her the naked truth. "I wish there was a way we could be together."

"So do I." She gazed up at him, anguish in her green eyes. "But I can't live back there anymore. I didn't know that for sure myself until after we'd...after..."

"After we'd made love." He dared to put that name on it, even if doing so would only make things worse.

"Yes." She hugged him closer. "I wanted to talk about my decision, but it never seemed like the right time. And then...I picked a *horrible* time. I'm so sorry, Michael."

He smiled, remembering the way she'd practically knocked him down with her passionate greeting in the backyard. "I liked the first part of that discussion."

"That's what was so wrong about it! First I attacked you like a crazed rock star groupie, and then I lowered the boom. That's twisted."

"You were only being honest. Just because you love my writing and kind of like me, too, that doesn't mean you should arrange your life around those things."

"A part of me wants to."

He slid his hands down to cup her bottom and squeezed. "I'll bet I know which part."

"No, you don't, smarty pants. Not that part. It's my—"

"Don't tell me." He looked into those green eyes and silently commanded her to hold her tongue. If she admitted that she felt the same way about him that he felt about her, they'd both be lost. "You know I have to go back."

"I know," she said quietly. "There's no better place to be if you're a bestselling author."

"And it's my home. My family's there. This has been a lot of fun, but I'm not a cowboy."

"Emily thinks you are."

"Was she the one you were talking to at the corral?"

Keri nodded. "She says you're a cowboy because you kept going even after humiliating yourself by grabbing the saddle horn."

"Good God. Is *that* the benchmark? Being humiliated and forging on, anyway?"

"According to Emily."

"I say she's full of it. A real cowboy wouldn't have been humiliated in the first place."

"That's where you're wrong, Michael. In the year I've worked at the Last Chance, I've seen cowboys humiliated all the time. They make stupid mistakes like the rest of us. But any cowhand worth his salt will laugh it off and keep going. Which you did today."

He gazed down at her. "Thank you for that. And while I'm at it, let me thank you for every wonderful thing you've done since I arrived—and there are dozens. You're a treasure, Keri Fitzpatrick, and I'm going to miss you like hell."

"You say that like you're leaving tonight. Have you changed your plans?"

"No, but under the circumstances, I wasn't sure how you wanted to handle everything going forward."

Her eyes took on an impish glow. "I'd like to handle them the same as always. Lovingly and often."

He groaned. "I am seriously going to miss you."

"How did *you* want to handle things going forward?"

He was tempted to echo her smart-aleck remark, but instead, he found himself confessing his original plan. "I'd intended to make tonight all about sex."

She wiggled against him. "That sounds promising."

"What I mean is, *only* about sex. No emotional involvement. Just raw sex, lots of orgasms, especially for you, and maybe even some kinky stuff thrown in, since I'll never see you again after this week."

"Kinky stuff? What kind of kinky stuff?"

"I hadn't decided." He peered down at her. "Don't tell me that whole scenario appeals to you?"

"Not the *whole* scenario, but you couldn't deliver that, anyway."

"Who says?" He wondered if she doubted the kinky part. He could come up with kinky if he wanted to, especially when inspired by a lusty woman like Keri.

"You couldn't have sex without emotional involvement, so don't even try it."

Oh. He sighed. "You're probably right. It sounded good when I was planning my strategy."

"But I'm intrigued with the idea of kinky sex."

He'd kept his cock under control until she said that. Now it rose to the occasion. "Let me see what I can do about creating something."

"It's our last night alone upstairs." She rubbed against him.

"I'm well aware of it. Are you aware that you're alone in the barn with a very aroused cowboy?"

"Yes." She eased out of his arms and backed away. "And I'm also aware that Jack and Gabe are waiting for us to finish our conversation so they can put the tack away and go home to their wives."

"Good point."

"But I really like the fact that you referred to yourself as a cowboy." She continued backing toward the open doorway. "That's progress."

"It was a slip of the tongue. I still have a long way to go."

"Maybe I can help you get a little closer tonight."

He fought down the urge to go after her and drag her into an empty stall. Gabe and Jack's dinner plans didn't seem like a priority right now. "How could you do that?"

"I'm not sure yet, but I have some time. I'll work on a few ideas. I'll see you upstairs around nine."

"I'll be a basket case by then."

"That's the idea." She blew him a kiss and left the barn.

He stood there, breathing fast and willing his erection to subside.

"Hey, Michael!" Jack's voice drifted from the open door. "We saw her leave. You decent?"

"If you're asking if I'm dressed, the answer is yes. If you're asking if I'm a kind and generous soul, the jury's still out."

"I figure you're as kind and generous as the rest of us around here." Jack walked down the barn aisle, the bucket of grooming supplies dangling from one hand. "How'd it go?"

"She wants kinky. Wait! Forget I said that. I don't know why I told you that!" Michael rubbed a hand over his face. "Jeez. I can't believe I blurted that out. I'm obviously losing it."

Jack seemed to find the subject hysterical. "You mentioned it because you know old Jack can give you some suggestions."

"No! Don't give me suggestions. I don't want to talk about it."

Jack shrugged. "Okay." He turned and started back down the aisle carrying the bucket.

"Like what?"

Jack turned back, his grin wide. "It's basic, but you can't go wrong with some thin strips of rawhide and a can of whipped cream."

"Where can I get the rawhide?"

Jack motioned toward the tack room. "There's a roll of it in there. Take what you need. As for the whipped cream, raid Mary Lou's refrigerator. Just don't let her catch you."

15

KERI HAD SOME concept of what a dance-hall girl should look like from watching movies. She had enough of an idea that she might be able to recreate it for Michael's benefit. She had one dress that sort of fit the bill. It was long, black and tight, with a slit in the skirt that reached midthigh. The neckline plunged a satisfying amount, too.

If the evening was as wild and lusty as she hoped, the dress would be ruined. She'd paid a small fortune for it, and heaven knew why she'd brought it with her to Jackson Hole. But in the new life she envisioned for herself she wouldn't need a dress like this ever again, so she might as well sacrifice it to a good cause.

She'd been afraid their last night alone up here would be filled with angst and regret, but as she dabbed perfume everywhere she could reach, she no longer feared that. Tonight they were going to celebrate who they were. They were going to play. And then they would have fabulous sex. They would end this affair on a high note.

She'd piled her hair into an elaborate updo and had

added a couple of fabric flower hair ornaments she'd also brought from Baltimore for some unknown reason. She wore an emerald necklace that she should have left in the safe back home and several rings that belonged in a bank vault. Anyone who didn't know would assume it was all costume jewelry.

Michael would know, of course, but they could pretend it was fake. To emphasize that idea, she'd put on more makeup than she'd worn since arriving in Wyoming. Eyeliner, mascara and green eye shadow, all applied with a heavy hand, made her look like a lady of the night. Hot red lipstick added to the image.

Under the dress she'd put on a black lace garter belt, sheer black stockings and nothing else. No bra, no panties. She would have killed for a pair of fishnet hose, but she didn't have any. As a final touch, she slipped into glittery silver heels that added a good two inches to her height.

Finally, knowing she was already ten minutes late, she opened her door and walked across the hall. He'd left his door slightly ajar. Heart pounding, she pushed it open.

He lounged in the room's single upholstered chair. He'd pulled it over to the bed, which he'd stripped of its comforter. Then he'd propped his booted feet on the dark green sheets, as if he didn't give a damn if he got them dirty or not. She'd bet he'd cleaned his boots before doing that, but still…the pose was effective.

He wore his hat pulled low and didn't look up when she entered. His shirt was open, baring his lightly furred chest. He'd discarded his belt and opened the top button of his jeans. He looked like an image from a fantasy cowboy calendar.

Moisture sluiced through her, and because she wore no panties it dampened her inner thighs. She pitched her voice low. "Hi, there, cowboy."

He lifted his head to gaze at her, his expression giving nothing away. "Howdy, ma'am."

She slid her hands over the smooth fabric covering her hips. "Want some company?"

"I might."

She ran her tongue over her ruby-red lips as she strolled over to his chair. When she propped her foot on the edge of the seat, the side slit fell open. It almost, but not quite, revealed all. "I'll make it worth your while."

"I do believe you will." Slowly he lowered his booted feet and uncoiled himself from the chair. His glance traveled from her silver heel, braced on the chair, up the length of her stocking-covered leg. His muted swallow was the only sign that she'd affected him at all.

She had to give him credit. He seemed cool as a cucumber, while her pulse was thrumming wildly out of control. She was breathing hard, too, which made the black silk over her breasts tremble.

He focused on her cleavage. "Nice dress."

"Just an old rag I found."

Reaching out, he trailed the back of his hand over the emerald necklace and down to the edge of the daring neckline. "An old rag?"

"Worthless."

"Then you won't care what happens to it, will you?" She lifted her chin. "Not a bit."

In one swift move, he grasped the front of her neckline and yanked down. The dress came apart as if made of tissue paper. She'd had no idea it was so fragile.

Now it really *was* an old rag that hung in tatters, allowing him to see her quivering breasts, the black garter belt, and a dark triangle of curls already damp and ready for him. If he looked closely, and he seemed to be doing that, he might notice her thighs were slick, too.

Stepping back, he surveyed his handiwork. "Lie down on the bed."

"Should I take off—"

"No. Like that. Exactly like that."

She stretched out on the quilt, glittering heels and all. As he walked toward the headboard, he pulled something from his back pocket and looped it around her wrist. It was a thin strip of leather that reminded her of the trendy bracelets for sale in Jackson.

But this wasn't a trendy bracelet. She gulped for air. He was tying her wrist to the bedpost. And she was going to let him.

MICHAEL HAD NEVER done anything like this in his life, and his cock was so hard from the excitement of it he wondered if it might crack from the strain. Keri made no protest as he tied her wrists to the bedposts.

Then he tied her ankles, which left her open to his greedy gaze. He could come just looking at her. She breathed in quick little pants that made her whole body quake. That was delicious by itself, but he was enthralled as he drank in the sight of her stocking-covered legs spread to reveal exactly how much she wanted him. He stood at the foot of the bed, concentrating on that view, while he stripped off his clothes.

When he finally freed his cock he groaned with relief. He was tempted to forget about the whipped cream and dive into the banquet she presented. But he'd braved Mary Lou's kitchen to steal a can of it, and not using it now would mean he'd wasted all that effort.

He'd wanted the whipped cream to be a surprise, so he'd tucked it under the bed. He reached for it now and Keri's eyes widened.

Then she began to laugh. "Oh, my God. You're going to be in big trouble with the housekeeper if you get that all over the sheets."

"It's okay. I'm planning to bribe the housekeeper."

"Oh?" Her green eyes sparkled as bright as the emeralds she wore. "With what?"

"She'll find out really soon." He smiled.

"You know, it takes guts to steal Mary Lou's whipped cream."

"Are you going to turn me in?"

"No, cowboy," she murmured. "I won't squeal on you."

"Thanks." He climbed onto the bed. "But you can squeal now, if you want." And he sprayed mounds of whipped cream on each breast.

She did squeal, and she pulled against her bindings. "That's so cold!"

"Then let me warm you up." By the time he'd cleaned all the whipped cream from her breasts, she was pulling at the leather for a different reason. And begging.

But he had more plans for the whipped cream. Leaving her writhing on the bed, he walked to the foot, climbed in between her spread legs, and aimed the can's nozzle.

"Michael! Don't you dare put that cold stuff on my—" She squealed again as he sprayed her liberally with sweet clouds of white. "Michael! Do something!"

"Oh, I plan to." He went to work, and she quickly seemed to forget about being cold. He'd figured on licking away all the whipped cream, but all he really wanted was her moist, juicy center, so when he reached that, he left the rest to decorate her thighs.

She was nearly ready to come, though, and he wanted to set her free before she did. She complained mightily as he interrupted his feast to untie her, but she'd thank him later when she didn't have rope burns. As he settled into position again, she clutched his head and held him exactly where she wanted him.

He thought that was only fair after the way he'd imprisoned her. Besides, he was more than happy to stay right there, doing exactly what they both wanted. She tasted like heaven. He didn't even care that she pulled on his ears when she came. Nothing mattered but loving her, and loving her some more, until she lay panting and spent on a very sticky sheet.

He kissed his way up her body. She was pretty sticky, herself. Finally he reached her red, red mouth and hesitated. "Will that lipstick come off on me?"

She dragged in air. "Probably."

"Ah, hell. I don't care. We're both going to be a hot mess when this is over." And he kissed her with all the passion in his heart. It was a memorable kiss to start with, blending as it did the distinct flavors of sex, lipstick, and whipped cream.

He sank into the kiss and eased down onto her sticky body. She was a whipped cream disaster, and something about that turned him on even more. Sex, he suddenly realized, shouldn't always take place between scrubbed and polished bodies on freshly laundered sheets.

Sex should also be wild and messy and sticky, and if it was connected with other sensual delights, like food, so much the better. He wished he'd brought other items from Mary Lou's refrigerator so he could smear those on Keri, too.

He continued to kiss her as he slapped a palm on the nightstand and located the condom he'd put there. His hands weren't as sticky as the rest of him, at least not yet. Much as he hated to interrupt this all-encompassing, very flavorful kiss, he had to do that if he wanted his own climactic reward.

And he did want it, desperately. He longed to merge with her in every way, with his lips, his tongue, his hands, his arms, his legs and, most of all, his cock. When he pushed forward and locked himself in tight, she sighed happily.

"Perfect," she said.

"I know." Covering her mouth with his once again, he pumped slowly, almost reverently. He'd never thought about it before, but opening herself to him was so very generous. She was letting him inside her body. No, not just *letting* him inside. She welcomed him there.

With each thrust, she lifted her hips to greet him. She wanted this connection as much as he did, and that was some sort of miracle, wasn't it? She was willing to be vulnerable with him. She'd allowed him to tie her up, for God's sake. And squirt her with whipped cream.

As he rocked easily back and forth, knowing that he would come, but not ready to rush the process because

he liked it too much, he faced the truth. He was in love
with her. Besides that, unless he was a lousy judge of
people, she was in love with him.

Right now, as they enjoyed their mutual passion in
this sticky bed, being in love was a wonderful thing.
Next week, when they weren't together anymore, it
might not be quite so wonderful.

The answer to that problem was blindingly simple.
He couldn't believe he hadn't thought of it before, but
sometimes the most obvious solutions were the easiest
to overlook. It would be all right. They would be okay.

With that issue solved, he gave himself up to the
power and glory of making love to Keri Fitzpatrick. Of
course they wouldn't end their relationship on Sunday.
That would be stupid. Michael was many things, but
stupid wasn't one of them.

"Acting on impulse is not a good idea." Keri sat in the
middle of the mess they'd made of the sheets as early
morning sunlight slowly brightened the room. She
couldn't believe what she'd just heard come out of Michael's mouth. "I know you're not stupid, so—"

"Thank you for that. I'm not stupid. Some have even
called me brilliant. And moving here is the smartest
idea I've ever had in my life."

She gazed at him as he paced the room wearing only
his jeans. He'd been awake since four and he'd spent
the time while she slept writing. The moment she'd
roused herself enough to realize he wasn't in bed with
her anymore, she'd sat up and discovered him typing
away at the small desk.

Although he'd seemed lost in his imaginary world,

he must have sensed that she was awake, because he'd shut down the computer. Then he'd told her that the ranch inspired him, and that *she* inspired him. He no longer wanted to live in New York City.

"You've been here less than a week," she said. "And you've lived in New York your entire life. What about your family? Your friends?"

He shrugged the broad shoulders that looked so damned good naked. "I'll visit them, or even better, they'll visit me. They all have plenty of money. Money shrinks distance between people."

She yearned to follow him into this fantasy, but one of them had to keep a clear head. "I think you have it backward. Stay in New York. Visit here. Give yourself some time to—"

"I don't need time. I need this place." His expression grew more intense. "I need you."

Oh, boy. She understood. She really did. They'd had some amazing sex, and she was falling for him, too. But that didn't mean he should abandon everything and everyone in his former life and move far from the center of the publishing world just to be with her.

She took a long, shaky breath. "I love hearing that you need me. But changing your entire life on the spur of the moment doesn't make sense."

"You did."

"Yes, but I…I wasn't coming here to be with someone. That puts more weight on the situation."

"And that scares you?"

"A little. You like Jackson Hole in August, but will you like it in February, when it's twenty below, not even counting the wind chill factor?"

He smiled. "We'll keep each other warm."

How she longed to sink into that smile, to believe in his vision of the future, to welcome this decision with the joy he obviously expected from her. But she couldn't do it. He could be setting them both up for a fall.

"Winter on a ranch in Wyoming is nothing like winter in New York City. You're sometimes cut off from the basics like food and gas. Keeping the animals warm is a constant concern."

He met her gaze. "I'm sure it's not New York, and I'm ready to experience the difference."

"Are you, really? It took me a year before I knew for sure this was where and how I wanted to live. You can't possibly—"

"You're wrong, Keri. I can feel the chains coming off with every breath I take. My family is so damned proud of their heritage, which dates back to the effing Mayflower. Leaving New York would be unthinkable for them. All my life I've bought the premise that Hartfords always live east of the Hudson. But I belong here. On some level I've always known that."

"You're so good with words." Her heart ached. "I would love to be convinced by that argument, but Michael, you don't really know what you're talking about. You arrived on Monday afternoon. This is only Friday morning. You've experienced a tiny sliver of life on this ranch during August. You need more time, more exposure to the seasons, and more exposure to living a rural existence."

He exhaled, obviously impatient with her stance. "I'm beginning to think you don't want me here, Keri."

"No, that's not it! Of course I want you here. I'm…

fond of you." If she mentioned the *L* word, that would only make things worse.

"Fond of me?" He studied her as if considering the meaning of that.

"Very fond." It was all she'd allow herself to say right now.

"If you're so *fond* of me, why are you throwing up these roadblocks?"

"I'm worried that you're making a rash decision that will turn out to be a huge mistake. If you move out here and discover it's not for you, then what?"

"That's not going to happen."

She was so afraid he was doing this mostly because of her, and changing an entire life for one person, especially one he'd known a few days, sounded like a recipe for disaster. "Okay, let me ask you this. If I changed my mind and decided to go back to Baltimore, would you still move here?"

His hesitation said it all.

"Please give this some more thought before you plunge ahead." She climbed out of bed. "You need to move here because it's the right place for you, not because you want to be with me. I shouldn't be your reason."

He looked as if he wanted to say something, but then he shook his head and turned away. "You're right." He walked over to the window and stared out at the mountains. "I sometimes let these flights of fancy get the best of me." His words sounded reasonable, but his tone and his body language were defiant.

If he'd looked at her while he'd admitted his impulsive nature, she might have believed that he intended to rein it in. Instead, he had his back to her, and what a rigid back it was, too.

Judging from his posture as he stood at the window, she didn't think he was calmly considering his options. She feared he was bitterly disappointed because she hadn't thrown herself into his arms and celebrated this wonderful decision with him.

It would have been so easy to do. And so unwise. "I need to get down to the kitchen."

"Yes, I know." He didn't turn around.

"Michael, I hope you understand why I didn't jump on your idea with cries of glee."

"I do."

"Well, good." She waited a moment longer to see if he'd turn around. Nope. "I'll see you downstairs," she murmured.

"See you then."

16

THE FIRST WEDDING guests, the O'Connelli family, arrived around ten on Friday morning. Michael had just finished grooming Destiny after a short trail ride on his own, a gratifying sign that at least Jack had confidence in him. Keri was another matter.

Besides giving the okay for a solo ride, Jack had also prepped Michael on the eccentric O'Connellis. He wasn't startled when a Volkswagen bus covered with peace signs and other New Age symbols pulled into the circular drive in front of the ranch house.

Free spirits Seamus O'Conner and Bianca Spinelli had combined their last names when they'd married in the seventies, creating the surname O'Connelli. Morgan, Gabe's wife, was one of seven O'Connelli siblings. Seamus and Bianca had arrived for Gabe and Morgan's wedding three years ago in this same bus.

The following year, another of the O'Connelli daughters, Tyler, had become Jack's sister-in-law when she'd married Alex Keller, Josie's brother. With two daughters living here, the vagabond O'Connellis had become regular visitors to the Last Chance.

Tyler's twin brother, Regan, had come for the wedding, and so had his seventeen-year-old sister, Cassidy. The four O'Connellis, who had spent a good part of their lives crammed into a Volkswagen bus, were apparently delighted to be given a room upstairs that included four bunks.

The other four-bunk room was reserved for Pete Beckett's two brothers and their wives, who often traveled together and were used to sharing quarters. The remaining room upstairs, a small one with a twin bed and a tiny attached bath, would go to Pete's aunt Georgia, who reportedly was quite spry for eighty-nine.

As people came rushing out of the house to greet the arrivals, Michael took Destiny out to the pasture and lingered there after he turned the horse loose. He wasn't in the mood to be social. Not just yet.

In the wee hours of the morning, when he'd thought that his life was finally beginning to make sense, he'd looked forward to the hustle and bustle of the wedding weekend because he and Keri would experience it together. Now he wished to hell he'd planned to leave today. Participating in the cheerful festivities wouldn't be easy after discovering that the woman he loved was merely *fond* of him.

Okay, maybe she was more than fond, but she wasn't willing to commit to what she was feeling, and she sure as hell hadn't leaped onboard with his new plan. Instead, she'd tried to talk him out of it with some ridiculous argument about extreme weather and the problems of rural living. As if any of that would matter to him if he could be with her.

He was a writer who spent hours alone in imaginary

settings. When he left those imaginary places and re-joined reality, having her there would be far more important to his happiness than whatever lay outside the door. But she'd told him to make his decision without factoring her into it.

He couldn't do that. He'd fallen in love with the place and the woman at the same time. Knowing that she wanted to stay here made for a perfect situation, if only she'd admit that she loved him as much as he loved her. He'd thought so last night, but now…well, if she wouldn't say it, why wouldn't she?

Maybe because she didn't want to be the reason he moved to the Jackson Hole area. But she was a huge part of it. If she'd been heading back to Baltimore, he wouldn't have considered moving here. Where she lived would factor into his decision, but he couldn't say the same about her. She'd been willing to end their relationship so that she could stay in Wyoming.

No matter which way he looked at her reaction to his plan, the conclusion remained the same. He was head over heels, and she was less so. That sucked.

But the Chances had been terrific to him ever since he'd arrived, and he would shake off this rotten mood and do his best to be upbeat for the next couple of days. Tonight everyone was headed to the Spirits and Spurs, the bar in Shoshone owned by Jack's wife, Josie. Michael had been invited a couple of days ago, but he'd begged off, saying that this was for family, not some stranger from back east.

His real reason, of course, had been that he'd hoped to spend time alone upstairs with Keri while the place was empty of guests. That wasn't such a good idea any-

more. Another night in bed with her, and he was liable
to make an even bigger fool of himself than he already
had. Might as well ask if he was still welcome at the
Spirits and Spurs tonight and see if he could forget his
troubles for a few hours.

BEING RIGHT WAS no fun at all. Keri believed with all her
heart that she'd done the right thing by trying to convince Michael to take his time. He was talking about
making such a drastic change. But she hated the distance she'd created between them.

And there certainly was distance. He'd avoided her
gaze when he'd come down for breakfast, and he'd left
with only a brief goodbye. Later, as she'd bundled up
the sticky sheets and remade his bed, she'd wondered
if they'd ever make love again. Something told her they
might not.

She'd put the sheets in with a load of towels and her
ruined dress was shoved into the depths of a garbage
bag. Their night of mildly kinky sex would remain a
secret, but she longed for a smile or a wink from Michael to let her know he remembered that part of the
evening and not just the awkward discussion that followed in the morning.

She'd tried to blame all the wedding activity for
keeping them from exchanging any private words, but
she knew that wasn't the reason. Lunch had been a cha-
otic affair with all the extra guests, but that should have
made it easier for him to find a moment to say something to her. No one would have noticed.

He'd made no effort to connect ever since she'd left
his room this morning, and she missed him more than

she could have imagined. Someday soon, after he'd left here and had given himself a chance to gain perspective, he'd realize that her advice had been good. But picturing that moment of clarity didn't keep her from feeling sad that they were estranged now.

She was fairly certain he hadn't planned to go to the Spirits and Spurs with the wedding party, but she wasn't surprised when he went, after all. She and Michael could have had some time alone upstairs while the others were partying, but apparently he hadn't wanted that.

After everyone was gone, she closed herself in her room and took a long hot shower. It didn't relax her as much as she'd hoped, but she put on some light flannel pajamas and climbed into bed. Her usual evening entertainment, reading a Jim Ford book, would only make her feel more unhappy, so she switched off the light.

Closing her eyes, she tried a few relaxation techniques with no success. Her brain insisted on replaying the events of the day. Judging from Michael's behavior since this morning, she could expect the same tomorrow, and then on Sunday he'd leave.

She couldn't let him do that without making one more attempt to reach an understanding. She decided to write him a note and put it on his pillow. Maybe he'd rip it to shreds, but she didn't know how else to let him know that she'd acted out of love.

No, she couldn't say that. If she mentioned love, he'd take that as a sure sign that he should move here. He wouldn't give himself time to think about the decision.

She'd have to find a way to indicate she cared about him without using the *L* word. She'd been in PR, for

God's sake. Although she wasn't a professional writer like Michael, she was no slouch with the English language.

But as she sat down with a pen and one of the monogrammed notecards her mother had sent her for Christmas, she struggled. She ruined three notecards before she finally came up with something that sort of worked. She read it over one more time to be sure.

> Dear Michael,
> My reaction to your plan seems to have greatly disappointed you and destroyed the friendship we had. But I still believe what I said—that a major decision like this needs to be considered from all angles. I didn't say that to be a wet blanket or because I don't care about you. I do care, and I want you to be happy.
> Yours,
> Keri

She'd debated a long time over how to sign off. She certainly wasn't going to say *with love* or anything mushy. *Yours* was a common closing, and didn't have to mean anything more than *at your service.* If it meant something more personal to her, he wouldn't have to know that.

Slipping the notecard into its cream-colored envelope, she tucked the flap inside and wrote his name on the front. Then she walked quickly across the hall to his door.

Her heart pounded with anxiety, even though she'd seen him leave with the others and was certain he wasn't there. As she opened the door and confirmed that, bittersweet memories made her sigh with longing. Last night when she'd walked in, he'd been waiting with rawhide strings and whipped cream. Tonight, he'd been eager to get away from her for a few hours.

He hadn't left any lights on, but the moon shining through the window allowed her to find the switch on the bedside lamp. Once she turned it on, she could see that the room was as neat as she'd left it this morning, as if he didn't want to cause her any extra trouble. Last night he'd been willing to spray whipped cream on the sheets.

In another two days, it would be even neater, because no one would be staying here. She probably shouldn't think about that. Michael might be keeping his distance, but at least he was still in the vicinity. She could catch glimpses of him here and there. Yes, she was pathetic, but he would never know that.

She leaned down to lay the envelope against the pillow sham. Then she changed her mind. Tonight Michael would get turn-down service.

Removing the decorative pillows, she folded back the sheets. Then she turned on the other bedside lamp. She left the envelope propped against the pillow on what had become his side of the bed when they shared it. As an afterthought, she pulled one of the lupine blossoms out of the vase she'd refreshed that morning, shook the water off the stem and laid that on top of his pillow. A peace offering.

If all that didn't convince him that she meant well, he wasn't going to be convinced. She went over their conversation this morning and tried to think of how it could have turned out better. Maybe if he'd offered his plan as a possibility instead of a certainty, she wouldn't have been so alarmed.

But he'd proclaimed his intention boldly, leaving no room for discussion. When she'd tried to initiate discussion, he'd been closed to other options. His comment of *you're right* had sounded almost belligerent. Sometime during the night he'd made up his mind and that was supposed to be the end of it.

She might have let him stumble on if she hadn't been so closely tied to his decision. But he wasn't just moving to Wyoming. He also was moving to be with her. If it turned out to be the wrong thing for him, he could break both their hearts. Smoothing the folded sheet one last time, she returned to her room.

Several hours later, after she'd finally dozed off, she heard everyone come back. Footsteps on the stairs, murmured conversation and muffled laughter were followed by calls of *good night*. Then, instead of one pair of feet coming down the hallway toward Michael's room, there were two. And one of them stumbled a bit.

"Almost there," said a male voice that was not Michael's.

"Thanks, buddy. 'Preciate it."

Keri squeezed her eyes shut. The crazy idiot had decided to drown his sorrows, which meant he'd feel like crap tomorrow.

"Glad to help out, dude." The voice sounded too young to be one of Pete's brothers or Seamus O'Connelli, so that left Regan, Tyler's twin. "You were a riot, tonight."

Michael chuckled. "Was I?"

"I've never seen anyone stand on a table and recite Shakespeare's sonnets while balancing a mug of beer on his head. You got into it."

"Know why I did that?" Michael asked.

"Can't imagine, but it sure was funny." A door creaked open.

"I'm in looove."

Keri gasped. Dear God, was he, really? No, probably not. He was drunk and didn't know what he was saying.

"Congratulations," Regan said. "Okay, a little more... there we go."

The rest of the conversation was lost to Keri as Regan helped Michael through the doorway and into the room. She lay in the darkness, pulse racing, while she lectured herself not to dwell on an offhand remark by someone who was plastered. No doubt he'd meant it as a joke, something to amuse his new friend Regan.

But what if he'd meant it? Liquor acted like a truth serum sometimes. But he still shouldn't move to Wyoming on the strength of that, should he? Even if he loved her, he might still hate living in Wyoming year-round. Then what? They'd have a mess.

Oh, but the very thought that he might actually love her...that hovered in her mind, a glittering possibility that she dared not believe in. If she reached for it, would it disappear?

A door creaked again, and footsteps retreated as Michael's rescuer headed for the far side of the second floor. Another door opened and closed far down the hall, and all was quiet except for the erratic thumping of her heart. She needed to go to sleep, but that wasn't going to happen anytime soon.

Eventually she turned on the light and picked up one of her Jim Ford books. Opening it to the back, she gazed at Michael's author photo for a long time. She'd always been drawn to his eyes, even in a small black-and-white picture. Those eyes seemed utterly sincere. They weren't the eyes of a man who would say something he didn't mean, even in a drunken stupor.

Yet as she started rereading the book, she remembered that this man had allowed his fans to believe he was a seasoned cowhand. She understood his reasons, but maybe he wasn't as sincere as he looked. Maybe he was capable of blurting out words of love he didn't mean.

She continued to read, captured as always by his effortless prose. The clean crisp sentences had been part of the charm of his books. His style had convinced her that he was, in fact, a cowboy because he sounded like one.

After she'd read a few pages, she was startled to hear Michael's door open again. His steps whispered along the floor, and she guessed he was navigating the hallway in his bare feet. He walked into the bathroom and closed the door. Seconds later, the shower came on.

The man she'd thought was passed out in a heap on his bed was awake and in the shower. Putting down the book, she listened while the shower ran. He'd been known to fall asleep in the bathtub. Would he fall asleep in the shower?

She was about to check on him when he turned off the water. Moments later, the bathroom door opened and he returned to his room. She relaxed a little. He couldn't be in very bad shape if he'd managed a shower.

Switching off her light again, she eased down under the covers. A cool breeze through her open window soothed her and she closed her eyes, determined to get some sleep. The next day would be busy and she couldn't afford to be tired.

The knock at her door was so soft that she wasn't sure if she'd heard it or imagined it. Then it came again.

Adrenaline pumped through her. Only one person would knock on her door at this time of the night. Sliding out of bed, she left the light off as she went to the door. She opened it slowly, and his slurred declaration of love rang in her head as she gazed at him.

He wore only his jeans, and his dark hair was still damp from the shower. He wasn't smiling. "I saw your light under the door when I came out of the bathroom," he said quietly. "I figured we woke you up, and I apologize for that." He sounded a little hoarse, but not particularly drunk anymore.

She took a quick breath. "Apology accepted."

"Hang on." He lowered his voice even more. "There are more apologies where that came from."

"Oh?" She looked into his eyes, but could read nothing there.

"I apologize for putting you on the spot about me moving here, and for being such an ass when you offered me some helpful advice. I realize now you had my best interests at heart."

She swallowed. "Are you saying that you'll give the idea more thought before doing anything?"

An emotion flickered in his eyes. They looked very gray tonight. "Depends on what you mean by *anything*."

"I mean—"

"Never mind." A hint of a smile touched his mouth. "I know what you mean. I promise to give the idea more thought, but right now there is something I'd like to do, with your permission." The flicker in his eyes became a gleam.

She'd seen that gleam before, and the implication made her tremble with excitement. "What's that?"

"I'd like to thank you for your note."

That threw her a little. "You're...you're welcome."

"No, I want to *really* thank you. May I come in?"

17

MICHAEL HELD HIS breath while he waited for her answer. He wasn't convinced that she was as invested in this relationship as he was. She might have decided by now that he was too moody and not worth the trouble of further involvement.

But she'd written him that note, turned back his sheets and placed a flower on his pillow. She might not love him as much as he loved her, but apparently she still cared about him a little. If she'd let him, he'd build on that.

Obviously she hadn't expected him to show up at her door. The flannel pj's covered in little bouquets weren't what women usually wore to entice a lover. They did entice him, all the same.

She glanced down the hall, as if considering the reality of all the people sleeping upstairs tonight.

"We'll be quiet," he murmured.

Her green-eyed gaze lifted to his, and mischief danced there. "Do you think that's possible?"

"In my world, anything is possible." He grimaced. What a cheesy line. "Okay, maybe not anything. This won't be a sexual marathon. I'm not up to it. I've had quite a bit to drink."

"I know."

"You do?" He had a horrible thought. He'd assumed their stumbling around had been what had woken her up, but they'd been talking, too, mostly about his sonnet reciting stunt, and then he'd said...oh, hell. "When Regan and I came in, could you hear what we—"

"Couldn't make out the words. Just heard you both laughing and mumbling some kind of nonsense."

Something in her expression told him that might not be strictly true, but he'd let it go. In his boozy fog, he'd assumed she was asleep until he'd glimpsed her light on after his shower.

But in spite of all his boorish behavior recently, she seemed to be in a forgiving mood. Smiling, she moved back from her door and opened it a little wider. "You can come in."

"Thank God." He stepped inside and closed the door behind him.

She'd left the light off, which might be better. Lights only alerted others to activity that was none of their business. In the cool silky darkness, he turned his attention to getting her naked.

"Nice pj's," he murmured as he worked at the buttons of her top. His coordination wasn't quite up to par.

"Let me." She gently pushed his hands aside and made short work of the buttons. "I wasn't expecting company tonight." Slipping her arms free, she let the top slide to the floor.

"I know." He cradled her breasts in both hands, once

again struck by her generosity. "After the snotty way I behaved today, you could have refused to accept any."

"But you see, I invited you." She arched into his caress and wound her bare arms around his neck. "On monogrammed stationery, no less."

"I noticed that." He nibbled on her bottom lip and fondled the breasts she thrust so eagerly into his hands. "What's the S stand for?"

"Sexy."

"Knowing you, I'd buy that." He brushed his thumbs over her tight nipples. "Knowing who your family is, I don't."

"Suzanne. My mother's name."

"Keri Suzanne Fitzpatrick." Leaning back, he looked into her eyes. They shone even in darkness, somehow gathering in the soft light flowing in from the window. "You said in your note that you wanted me to be happy."

"I do."

"Making love to you would make me very happy."

"Me, too." Unwrapping her arms from around his neck, she reached down and untied the ribbon holding her pj bottoms. They fell to the floor. "So let's."

His cock twitched. Considering all the beer he'd consumed tonight, he'd wondered if he'd be able to get it up at all. He'd planned to focus on her and not worry about whether he could fully participate.

He followed that plan. After shucking his jeans, he guided her down to the bed and revisited his favorite places. He spent more time visiting some than others, and she was obliged to cover her face with a pillow to muffle her cries of release.

In the process, he discovered that there was life in his

cock, after all. Fortunately he was an optimistic kind of guy, and he'd shoved a condom in the pocket of his jeans. She had to find it, though. His coordination continued to be a little questionable.

He also required her help in putting on the little raincoat. Consequently, he decided against trying any fancy positions. Besides, the missionary had lots of pluses going for it, in his opinion. He'd never understood why it had a reputation for being boring.

Braced above her, he slid inside the warm sheath of her body with gratitude and joy. He wasn't even slightly bored. Then he kissed her, and she kissed him back. Yes, she definitely liked him. A woman who kissed with that much enthusiasm wasn't indifferent.

But he'd scared her this morning with his news, and he'd take that as a lesson learned. If he wanted her, and he did, then he had to behave like a rational human being. Then maybe she'd believe that he loved… ah…so sweet…loved everything about her…mmm… especially…most especially…this.

KERI HADN'T SLEPT much, but the next day she drew energy from knowing that she and Michael had mended the rift between them. Whatever the future might bring, at least on this special day of Sarah and Pete's wedding, they would enjoy that unspoken connection that had united them from the moment they'd met.

The morning and early afternoon passed in a blur. Then, before anyone was quite ready for it, they had less than an hour before the ceremony. Keri and Mary Lou shooed everyone away so they could shower and change.

Then the two of them tucked any remaining wild-flowers in vases and straightened the rows of white folding chairs arranged in the living room. All the furniture had been stacked in the backyard and covered with a tarp, although the sky remained clear.

Mary Lou adjusted the white satin runner that defined the center aisle. Then she walked to the back of the room and stood, arms folded. "Beautiful."

"It is." Keri shifted one bouquet of flowers on the hearth, which was a mass of red, yellow and purple wildflowers. "There. Perfect."

"Sarah married Jonathan in this room," Mary Lou said.

"She did? Does Pete know that?"

Mary Lou nodded. "He's the one who suggested they have the ceremony here. I've never met a man who's less jealous of the guy who preceded him. I never thought Sarah would find someone who could measure up to Jonathan, but Pete...well, he's just special."

"I agree." Keri walked around the chairs to stand next to Mary Lou. "You know why this looks so wonderful?"

"The wildflowers," Mary Lou said.

"That's a big part of it, but I think it's beautiful because it was created with love by Sarah's daughters-in-law. I watched Dominique, Morgan and Josie work together. Then Tyler showed up to help, and Bianca O'Connelli, and Emily."

"Don't forget Cassidy," Mary Lou said with a chuckle. "She's a seventeen-year-old ball of fire. I loved how eager she was to help do whatever we needed.

She'd race to get string, vases, duct tape, with her red hair flying."

"Yep, she's a cutie. I think she's after my job."

"She's young, but she's a hard worker, and according to her mother she isn't set on going to college, at least not yet." Mary Lou glanced over at Keri. "How soon are you planning to leave?"

Keri decided she could confide in Mary Lou, so she described the job she hoped to create working with Bethany Grace. "And Jack said it's a great idea, and he'll put in a good word with Bethany when she gets home. He's almost positive she doesn't have anybody hired for that position."

"That's terrific!" Mary Lou's face lit up. "So you'd be right next door, so to speak."

"I would."

"Okay, now I don't feel so sad about you leaving. I think you'll get that job with Bethany and then you'll be over at the Triple G, and we'll see you all the time."

Keri's heart squeezed. She hadn't realized that she'd be so missed. "Now I'm even more determined to convince Bethany to hire me."

"Well, if you need a reference, send her straight to me."

Keri smiled. "Thank you. I will."

"Now let's make sure all's well in the kitchen. We don't have much time left."

Keri followed Mary Lou back to the kitchen and they worked until it was nearly time for the ceremony. After tidying themselves as best they could, they walked back to the living room. Many of the chairs were already filled. They stood to one side and waited until the other guests had been seated before slipping into a spot in the back row, which had been provided for the ranch hands. The boss lady was getting married, and no one could be left out. By a stroke of luck, Michael was also in the back, and he took advantage of the vacant chair to Keri's right.

Watkins and the new hire, Trey Wheeler, played old country favorites as the guests settled themselves. Trey had turned out to be a top-notch horse trainer and a fine musician. Having two guitars instead of one provided a more resonant sound and had been a good decision, in Keri's estimation. During the ceremony, Tyler would add her talented voice to the guitar music.

Watkins and Trey made an interesting combination. Watkins was stocky, mustached and middle-aged, while Trey was young, lean, and muscled. Keri noticed with amusement that most of the women in the room watched Trey instead of Watkins, even though Watkins was a better guitar player.

Pete, who stood by the hearth with his two brothers and the minister, looked as if he'd won the lottery. Any minute Keri expected him to levitate.

As excitement grew, Watkins and Trey launched into "Here Comes the Bride." First down the aisle was the tiny flower girl, Morgan's daughter, Sarah Bianca, or SB for short. She flung rose petals everywhere, even pausing to launch them into the faces of the guests leaning toward her with cameras raised.

Mary Lou put her mouth next to Keri's ear. "Did you bring tissues? I'm going to bawl. I just know it."

Keri dug in her pocket and came up with one she handed to Mary Lou while keeping a second one for herself. She'd expected to cry. Sure enough, when Sarah appeared, flanked by her three handsome sons, Keri's tears began to flow. Regal as always, Sarah wore a long, ice-blue dress and carried a bouquet of the orchids Pete had ordered flown in from Hawaii. She was radiant.

Jack, Nick and Gabe wore ice-blue vests under their Western-style jackets. Sarah linked arms with Nick on one side and Gabe on the other, while Jack walked protectively behind. Each man's jaw was clenched against the emotion glittering in his eyes. All three had lived through the loss of a father and now manfully celebrated their mother's happiness in finding someone to love.

But Keri had come to know the Chance boys, and she didn't think they were giving Sarah away. They would never do such a thing. It was more of a provisional loan that depended on Pete's ability to keep her deliriously happy.

Judging from Pete's expression when he caught his first glimpse of Sarah, he was more than ready to do that. He looked as if he wanted to rush forward and escort her to the altar himself. But he wisely refrained. Those three broad-shouldered cowboys would have stopped at nothing to keep him from interfering in this special moment with their beloved mother.

By the time each of them had embraced Sarah and stepped back, there wasn't a dry eye in the house. Keri dabbed at her tears with her left hand, because her right hand was now clutched in Michael's left. She had no idea when he'd taken hold of her hand, but he didn't seem about to let it go.

She didn't mind. Holding on to him during this emotional ceremony felt good and right, so long as neither of them attached too much significance to it. And yet, that wasn't so easy as Sarah and Pete pledged to love and cherish each other.

Their promises were heartfelt, but Keri reminded herself that Sarah and Pete were rooted in this place and had been for years. They knew exactly what they were doing by creating this union. They were grounded in reality, not banking on some half-baked dream to carry them through.

Keri tried to keep that in mind, but the ceremony was magic, and some of the fairy dust fell on all of them. Looking at Pete and Sarah, it was hard to refute the power of love, or the belief that, as Michael had said, anything was possible.

When the vows had been said and the minister invited Pete to kiss the bride, the room erupted in cheers and applause. Keri joined in. She was so glad she'd stayed for this. As the jubilant couple turned and hurried down the aisle, Michael caught Keri's chin and turned her in his direction.

"Thank you for sharing this with me," he murmured right before he kissed her. The kiss was brief, but potent nonetheless.

She hadn't expected it, and she looked up at him, a little dazed. "I have to go. Mary Lou needs help in the kitchen."

"I know." He smiled and traced her mouth with the tip of his finger. "But you can come to the reception later, right?"

"Sarah told us to. She doesn't want anyone missing the party."

"Then save me a dance." He squeezed her hand and

before she could say anything about that, he was gone, swallowed by the crowd following Sarah and Pete out the door to the tents set up for the reception.

The next two hours flew by, with Mary Lou, Keri and a couple of extra servers hired for the occasion making sure the buffet tables were stocked and the bar well supplied. Keri was dressed for practicality in jeans, a T-shirt and a serviceable apron. Party clothes hadn't been part of the plan. She hadn't stayed on at the Last Chance so she could party tonight. She'd stayed so that Sarah could have a fabulous wedding free of worries about her staff.

But then Watkins appeared with strict instructions from the boss lady. Tyler's husband, Alex, a former DJ, had taken over the music duties, so Watkins had been commissioned to get Mary Lou out on the dance floor. Rumor had it that Michael was searching for Keri for the same reason.

She was carrying a kettle of ranch beans when Michael found her. He took it gently from her hands, set it on the nearest sturdy surface, and reached behind her to untie her apron.

"This is ridiculous," she protested. "I'm a part of the staff, not a part of the guest list."

Michael pulled her apron off and tossed it next to the kettle of beans. "I have my orders from Sarah. If I don't get you out there for at least one dance, she'll send all three of her boys to carry you to the dance floor. I doubt you want that."

Keri laughed. "No, I don't. I'm familiar with public embarrassment, and it's not all it's cracked up to be."

"Then you'll come along like a good girl?"

"I'll come along, but I can't promise that I'll be a good girl."

Michael glanced at her over his shoulder as he tugged her toward the wooden platform. "Even better."

As it turned out, when they stepped onto the dance floor, Alex had cued up "The Heart Won't Lie," sung by Reba McEntire and Vince Gill. With a sense of inevitability, Keri moved into Michael's arms.

They danced, snuggled close together as the words about love and loss flowed around them. How easy it would be for her to murmur in his ear and say that she wanted him to move to Wyoming, that she wanted to be with him and that she loved him.

She resisted. She refused to do or say anything that would influence him in this so-very-important decision. One word from her, and he'd abandon his promise to think it through.

He rested his cheek against hers, and a few times he turned his head to press his lips to the soft spot beneath her ear. "I could stay like this forever," he murmured.

At times like this she felt the same way, but no matter how sweet it sounded, neither of them could stay like this forever. She'd come to realize that he was a romantic. Romantics sometimes talked that way, which wasn't a problem until they started believing it, too.

_18_

MICHAEL CARRIED THE sweetness of their dance at the reception with him for the rest of the evening. Neither of them made it upstairs until well past midnight, and he knew she had to be exhausted. But it was their final night together, and he had to hold her one last time.

So he coaxed her into his room, gave her a massage, because this time she was the one who needed it, and made slow, gentle love to her until she came apart in his arms. Then he swallowed her cries so the others staying upstairs wouldn't hear.

Perhaps he'd hoped that the combination of the emotional wedding and good sex would change her opinion that he needed to proceed with caution. If so, he didn't get his wish. Her actions were loving, but she didn't beg him to move to Wyoming ASAP so they could be together.

But at least they shared a bed on their last night together. Without knowing for sure how deep her feelings ran, he couldn't say if that would ever happen again. He might come back in two months and discover that she'd fallen for a real cowboy.

That kind of thinking could easily drive him crazy, but he couldn't force her into a commitment she considered premature. Difficult though it would be, he had to leave her here, take care of business in New York and then see if he had anything to come back to.

She left his room early on Sunday morning. Although he knew that cleanup duties would be massive today, letting her walk out the door was torture. He stopped himself from asking for one more kiss and watched her cross the hall, her robe tied tight in case anyone else was up.

He'd bet no one was. Last night had been a blow-out of a party. God, but he hated to leave. If not for the damned video, he wouldn't. But filming was scheduled for next week, and he'd come to the Last Chance specifically to prepare for that.

So he packed, went down for a light breakfast and then headed to the barn so he could say goodbye to Destiny, his main guy, and Finicky, the superstar who'd let him pretend to know what he was doing. Keri must have spotted him going there, because he hadn't been in the barn talking to Destiny more than five minutes before she showed up.

"I thought we should say our goodbyes now, when nobody's around." She came toward him dressed in her usual outfit of jeans and a scoop-necked T-shirt. This one was the color of her emerald-green eyes.

"That's probably a good idea."

"Or silly. Most everyone has guessed about us."

"Must be the constant grin on my face." He met her halfway. As he slipped his arms around her waist, he couldn't banish the thought that he had no guarantees with this woman. He might never hold her this way again.

She gazed up at him. "Are you growing a mustache?"

"I am. For the video. You might not want to kiss me and risk razor burn."

"Why not admit who you are and forget about the mustache?"

"Because…" He stared at her in stunned silence. "I have no idea why not," he said at last. "That's an excellent question."

"You didn't want anyone to know before because you weren't a real cowboy, but you're a good part of the way there. You can pull it off."

"I suppose I could. Of course, my family will have a fit if I out myself as a Hartford of the Hudson Valley Hartfords." As he said that, he realized he no longer cared. He'd been willing to break with family tradition and leave New York, so why not go all the way?

Yet he hadn't been prepared to do that until now, and maybe that was a reason, a very good reason, she'd accused him of not thinking things through. If he intended to make Wyoming his home, then he should get rid of all the hang-ups from his past.

Her green eyes filled with understanding. "It's not easy to disappoint your family. Trust me, I know this."

"I know you do." And he had more work ahead of him in building an authentic life if he expected to deserve her. He already had some ideas about how he could do that. "Listen, can I send you a copy of the video after it's finished?"

"I'd love that. Is Jack driving you to the airport?"

"Yeah, he insisted."

"Then I'll give Jack my Baltimore address before you leave, so you'll have it."

"Baltimore?" He hoped to hell she hadn't been playing him like a fish. "Lady, you have me totally confused. Why am I sending the video to Baltimore?"

"Sorry, didn't mean to be confusing. I'm planning to talk with Jack in the next day or two and give my notice."

"Wow, that's quick."

"I'm impatient to get on with my plans. Bethany and Nash will be home from their honeymoon next week, and I don't want to risk having her hire somebody else to do the job I'm angling for."

He nodded. "Smart thinking."

"If all goes as I hope, I'll be in Baltimore tying up loose ends when your video's finished. I don't want you to send it here, because I want to see it right away."

"Glad to hear that. I have a feeling all of this will work out exactly the way you want it to." If only she'd factor him into her plans, he could talk about his goal of moving here. But that might make her freak out again, and they'd reached a kind of détente on that subject.

"I think it will, too. Mary Lou's excited that I might only be moving as far as the ranch next door. I was touched that she cared so much."

"I'm sure everyone will be rooting for you to get the job with Bethany. I know I am."

"Thanks, Michael." She gazed up at him. "I know you are, too."

He sighed and pulled her closer. "I don't want to say goodbye."

"Then don't." She reached up and cupped his face

in both hands. "Just kiss me, and then I'll walk out of here. No drama."

"Right. No drama." Leaning down, he closed his eyes and pressed his mouth to hers. His heart jerked in his chest. This could not be the last time he kissed her. It just couldn't.

She answered his kiss with tenderness. Then she eased out of his arms and turned. Without another word, she walked out of the barn. Everything that mattered to him went with her.

MICHAEL'S VIDEO ARRIVED shortly after Keri returned to her Baltimore condo, so she was doubly glad she'd asked him to send it there. It came via FedEx, and she nearly destroyed the packaging in her haste to get it out of the box. Then she fumbled with the disc as she attempted to load it into her player. Apparently this separation had made her desperate for the sight of Michael James Hartford, aka Jim Ford.

By the time she put the disc in the machine and hit Play on her remote, she was hyperventilating and couldn't even sit down to watch it. She stood right in front of the screen, the remote clutched so tightly in her hand that her fingers grew numb. If she'd thought his presence in her life wasn't important, she'd been kidding herself.

The segment started with a book cover that faded to an almost identical scene of rolling hills punctuated by a single tree with a hangman's noose dangling from it. Michael had recorded the voiceover describing the dramatic scene as it played out in the book.

Hearing that deep familiar baritone gave her goose

bumps. She had the fierce urge to see him in person. She needed to touch him and verify that he still existed in her world.

The video continued, and Michael came riding over the hill. Her reaction was immediate and visceral. The tug deep within her soul proclaimed that *this* man was the one she was meant to love.

To hell with logic. To hell with everything except a primitive need to eliminate whatever distance, emotional or geographical, separated them.

Then he began to speak, and she became a little shaky. She slowly lowered herself to the floor while she kept her attention focused intently on the screen. He looked into the camera, but he seemed to be gazing directly at her.

She realized that was the intent, and each viewer would feel as if he spoke directly to them. Well, they could all harbor that delusion, but she knew the truth. He was talking to *her,* damn it!

At first she didn't notice that he'd forsaken the mustache because he looked the way he always had, clean shaven. But the mustache was supposed to be part of his Jim Ford persona, or it had been until now.

"I have a confession to make," he said. *"Last week I learned to ride a horse and throw a rope. Until then, I'd been a city boy who wrote about things I'd dreamed of but never experienced."*

Her jaw dropped. In their last conversation, she'd casually asked him why he didn't reveal who he really was, but she hadn't expected him to tell everyone he hadn't been a cowboy before and was just becoming one now. Admitting that took nerve.

He continued, *"Last week opened my eyes to new possibilities and new challenges. I'm relocating to Wyoming so I can live the way I've always hoped to. I'll write under my real name, but I'll also keep Jim Ford somewhere on the cover of the books until everyone's adjusted to the change, including me. Oh, and I'm ditching the mustache. It interferes with kissing pretty women. And there's one in particular I look forward to kissing."*

He followed that with a smile so full of optimism and joy that it broke her heart. He'd told her of his long-term goals, and she'd had no faith in his ability to make a decision that fast. She'd been privileged to be the first to know, and she'd tried to talk him out of being extremely smart and very brave.

Fortunately, he'd ignored her advice and was barreling ahead with the courage of his convictions. Perhaps it was time for her to admit that not everyone needed time to think through a major life change. Some people, like Michael, were blessed with imagination and the insight that allowed them to see clearly when the right path opened up before them.

And she loved him for being so exceptional in that regard. She loved him for many other reasons, too. She just plain loved him, and it was time she told him so.

MICHAEL CURSED WHEN the apartment security guard called on the house phone to say a visitor was in the lobby. He'd been struggling with a scene in his new book and he'd nearly figured it out. Whoever it was could come back later when he wasn't writing.

"Tell them I'm not available, Jake," Michael cut in

before Jake could say who the visitor was. It didn't matter. It could be the Queen of England for all he cared. He had a scene to wrestle with and he was so close to making it work. "Have them come back tomorrow around ten."

That's what a security person in the lobby was there for, to screen anyone wishing to visit the building's occupants. Michael cherished that about the place and made regular use of the service.

"All right."

A minute later, Jake called again.

Michael considered not answering. He'd have to discuss this with Jake later and let him know that no meant no. Luther, the previous security person, had been very good at getting rid of unwanted visitors. But Jake had only been on the job a couple of months. Michael would have to answer and get rid of this persistent person himself.

"The young lady is prepared to wait in the lobby until you see her, Mr. Hartford."

"Look, she needs to come back tomorrow, Jake. Please convince her that—"

"Her name is Keri Fitzpatrick."

Michael's brain stalled. Disbelief was quickly followed by hope, followed by caution. She'd told him she'd be in Baltimore for a month, which was why he'd sent the video there.

But she'd never said anything about getting together while she was in Baltimore. She could have, but she hadn't, so he'd resigned himself to not seeing her, even though they would be just a train ride apart for the duration.

Maybe this was a spur-of-the-moment thing. Maybe she had business in New York and had stopped by for old time's sake. He shouldn't expect that this visit would have any special significance.

"Mr. Hartford? Shall I send her up?"

"Yes, send her up."

Even though he told himself not to get excited about seeing her, his heart pounded wildly as he waited for her to arrive at his door. He took several long slow breaths in an attempt to appear calm. Then the doorbell chimed, and his heart clicked into double time again.

Still, he did his best to look casual when he opened the door and found her standing there in her little black suit and four-inch heels. "Keri! It's good to—"

"I love you."

He opened his mouth to respond, but nothing would come out. His brain had turned to mush and the rest of him wasn't holding up well under the shock, either. He was afraid he was shaking.

"I love you, Michael," she said again. "I didn't want to say it while we were in Wyoming, because I had this stupid idea that I could ruin your life."

He wasn't aware that he'd moved, but suddenly he was holding her and kissing her with wild abandon as emotions he'd kept dammed up for weeks burst free. At last, gasping for breath, he lifted his head to gaze into her sparkling green eyes. "The only way you can ruin my life is by staying out of it. As it happens, I love you, too." And with that, the shaking stopped, as if when he proclaimed his love, his world had settled into place.

She smiled and wound her arms around his neck.

"So that wasn't just the booze talking when you were stumbling down the hallway?"

"So you heard that." He wasn't sure whether to be upset or grateful that she had.

"I did hear it." She looked into his eyes and let him see the love in hers. "Which reminds me. I'd like to do something, with your permission."

"What's that?"

"I'd like to thank you for making that video."

He started to grin. "You're welcome."

"No, I mean I *really* want to thank you. May I come in?"

Joy radiated through him. "You may. In fact, I insist." Sweeping her up in his arms, he carried her over the threshold and kicked the door shut behind them.

"That felt sort of symbolic."

"Oh, it was extremely symbolic." He smiled down at her. "You realize we'll have to plan quickly if we want to get married in the Last Chance living room before the snow flies."

"We can do it." Not a single doubt lingered in those green eyes. "As a very smart man once said, anything is possible."

Epilogue

TREY WHEELER HAD learned that winter could arrive in the Jackson Hole area anytime after the first of September. So he wasn't surprised when Emmett Sterling, foreman at the Last Chance, asked Trey and Watkins to clean and oil the tack in preparation for putting most of it away for the season.

Trey welcomed the job. He enjoyed working in the old barn, which had stood on the property for more than a hundred years. He craved that kind of tradition because he had so few of his own. He also liked Watkins. Not only was Watkins a top hand, he'd greatly improved Trey's guitar skills.

He and Watkins got along, and they hadn't been able to sit and talk since Pete and Sarah's wedding. Cleaning and oiling tack would give them that opportunity. The afternoon was cool, but they were cozy inside the barn, surrounded by the wholesome smell of horses and leather.

"So how did you like playing at a wedding?" Watkins picked up a bridle and began inspecting it for any places in need of repair.

"I liked it." Trey used saddle soap to clean one of

the working saddles that had seen plenty of use and abuse this summer from those crazy adolescent boys. Trey had been hired on in the middle of that session. He'd been working at a newer ranch closer to Jackson, but he'd always hoped something would open up at the Last Chance, and here he was, in a historic barn, cleaning tack.

"That's good, because they want us to provide the music for another one."

"Sign me up. I'm ready. Whose is it?"

Watkins chuckled. "Emmett's. But don't discuss this with him, because he's expecting something small. Or let's say, he's praying for something small."

"I take it Pam's not going along with that?" Trey had come on board soon after Emmett had proposed to Pam Mulholland, who owned a bed-and-breakfast down the road.

According to the gossip Trey had picked up since then, Emmett had been dragging his heels because Pam's wealth intimidated the hell out of him. Then a rival had come to town, and Emmett had been forced to put up or shut up.

"Pam was married to a real bastard. Now she finally has the love of her life, and she doesn't want some quiet ceremony with a couple of witnesses. She's rented out the entire Serenity Ski Lodge for the second weekend in December."

"Holy shit." Trey stopped in mid-motion. "That must have cost a small fortune."

"I'm sure it did, but Pam has a large fortune, and she wants a large party. I don't think Emmett's been given very many details, though, because she doesn't want him to freak out. So just keep this under your hat."

"But we're supposed to play at this ritzy lodge?"

"Yes, we are. Pam liked what she heard from us at Sarah and Pete's shindig, and she wants more of the same. She's already booked our rooms, and she's paying us, besides."

"Aw, hell, Watkins. She doesn't have to do that. We'll play for free, especially if we're getting a vacation out of it."

"She insisted, and threatened to turn into bridezilla if we didn't take the money. She—uh, never mind. Here comes Emmett. Mum's the word."

Emmett sauntered over, a piece of straw stuck in the corner of his mouth. He leaned casually against the wall and gazed at Watkins and Trey. "Did I hear you talking about my wedding?"

Watkins glanced up, his expression filled with innocence. "We were just discussing how happy we are for you."

Emmett chewed on the straw for a while before taking it out of his mouth. "Pam's up to something. I'm not sure what, yet, but I'll bet Mary Lou knows." He stared pointedly at Watkins.

"She might." Watkins picked up a rag and began oiling the bridle. "You could ask her."

"I was thinking you could ask her, considering you're married to her."

Watkins glanced up from his work. "She might tell me, but then she'd have to kill me."

Emmett sighed. "Okay. I'll go right to the source."

"Mary Lou?"

"No, Pam."

Watkins kept polishing the bridle. "Good luck with that."

"Thanks. I'll need it." Emmett glanced at Trey. "Take my advice, son. Don't fall in love. It gets you into all kinds of trouble."

Trey smiled at him. "I'll remember that." But Emmett's advice had come too late. Trey was already in love, and he didn't even know her name.

* * * * *

COMING NEXT MONTH FROM

Available August 20, 2013

#763 THE CLOSER • *Men Out of Uniform*
by Rhonda Nelson

Former ranger Griff Wicklow mastered the art of removing a woman's bra in high school, but protecting one worth two million dollars is another matter altogether. Especially when the real gem is the jeweler along for the ride....

#764 MISSION: SEDUCTION • *Uniformly Hot!*
by Candace Havens

Battle-scarred marine Rafe McCawley is in need of relaxation, but when he meets gorgeous pro surfer Kelly Callahan in Fiji, resting is the last thing on his mind!

#765 MYSTERY DATE
by Crystal Green

A woman craving sensual adventure. A lover who hides his identity in the shadows. An erotic interlude that takes each of them farther than they've ever dared to go....

#766 THE DEVIL SHE KNOWS
by Kira Sinclair

One incredible night with a mysterious bad boy in a red silk mask—that's all Willow Portis wants. Too bad she doesn't recognize her devil until it's too late....

REQUEST YOUR FREE BOOKS!
2 FREE NOVELS PLUS 2 FREE GIFTS!

HARLEQUIN®

Blaze®

red-hot reads!

YES! Please send me 2 FREE Harlequin® Blaze™ novels and my 2 FREE gifts (gifts are worth about $10). After receiving them, if I don't wish to receive any more books, I can return the shipping statement marked "cancel." If I don't cancel, I will receive 4 brand-new novels every month and be billed just $4.74 per book in the U.S. or $4.96 per book in Canada. That's a savings of at least 14% off the cover price. It's quite a bargain. Shipping and handling is just 50¢ per book in the U.S. and 75¢ per book in Canada.* I understand that accepting the 2 free books and gifts places me under no obligation to buy anything. I can always return a shipment and cancel at any time. Even if I never buy another book, the two free books and gifts are mine to keep forever.

150/350 HDN F4WC

Name	(PLEASE PRINT)	
Address		Apt. #
City	State/Prov.	Zip/Postal Code

Signature (if under 18, a parent or guardian must sign)

Mail to the Harlequin® Reader Service:
IN U.S.A.: P.O. Box 1867, Buffalo, NY 14240-1867
IN CANADA: P.O. Box 609, Fort Erie, Ontario L2A 5X3

Want to try two free books from another line?
Call 1-800-873-8635 or visit www.ReaderService.com.

* Terms and prices subject to change without notice. Prices do not include applicable taxes. Sales tax applicable in N.Y. Canadian residents will be charged applicable taxes. Offer not valid in Quebec. This offer is limited to one order per household. Not valid for current subscribers to Harlequin Blaze books. All orders subject to credit approval. Credit or debit balances in a customer's account(s) may be offset by any other outstanding balance owed by or to the customer. Please allow 4 to 6 weeks for delivery. Offer available while quantities last.

Your Privacy—The Harlequin® Reader Service is committed to protecting your privacy. Our Privacy Policy is available online at www.ReaderService.com or upon request from the Harlequin Reader Service.

We make a portion of our mailing list available to reputable third parties that offer products we believe may interest you. If you prefer that we not exchange your name with third parties, or if you wish to clarify or modify your communication preferences, please visit us at www.ReaderService.com/consumerschoice or write to us at Harlequin Reader Service Preference Service, P.O. Box 9062, Buffalo, NY 14269. Include your complete name and address.

HB13R2

SPECIAL EXCERPT FROM

HARLEQUIN

Blaze

Enjoy this sneak peek at

Mission: Seduction

by Candace Havens, part of the
Uniformly Hot! series from Harlequin Blaze

Available August 20, 2013,
wherever Harlequin Books are sold.

"I'm a pro." Kelly laughed. "I surf professionally. At least, I did until a few months ago when I hit Pause and bought this place."

If she'd earned enough to afford this luxury resort, she must have done well as an athlete.

Rafe chastised himself for staring at her, but stopping wasn't an option. He searched his brain to remember what they'd been talking about. "Why'd you hit Pause?"

"To reevaluate, decide what to do next with my life. Burnouts happen and to be honest, I was heading that way. I forgot my love for surfing and I wanted to remember why I've been so dedicated for so long. And it's helped. I can't wait for my next meet." She pursed her lips. "Listen to me. I sound like some weirdo trying to find herself."

"No, you don't," Rafe said quickly. "I love being a marine, but there are days I want to give it up and be a farmer or something."

She grinned. Her amusement pleased him. "You don't seem like the farmer type."

"That *would* be funny, since I've never been on a farm before," he admitted. "But, you know, a job where you work

HBEXP79768

with your hands and you're alone out in nature. No one's giving orders, and you don't have to constantly watch your back."

That was true. After his last assignment, he'd begun to reevaluate what was important to him. Unlike Kelly, he had no idea what might be next. His friend's private security company was his safety net.

But Rafe seldom took the safe path. His beat-up leg was proof of that.

"How did you end up here? Seems like a lot for one person to take on."

"I was always visiting during my time off because the waves are so great. A friend of mine owned it. One day he said he wanted to sell Last Resort, and everything fell into place so easily that I knew it was the right decision. It's a lot of work, but manageable for the most part.

He studied her for a moment. She was proud of what she'd accomplished, and she should be. From what he'd seen so far, this was about as close to paradise as one could get.

"So, dinner?"

"Oh, thanks for reminding me." She grabbed her board from where it'd been standing and tucked it under her arm. "Starts at seven, and it's very casual. Well, see ya tonight." She swung away with a jaunty lift to her step.

His gaze locked on her bikini-clad body sprinting up the beach. The woman was insanely beautiful in a doesn't-need-any-makeup, girl-next-door sort of way. It wasn't fair.

He laughed.

What was paradise without a little temptation?

Pick up MISSION: SEDUCTION by Candace Havens, available August 20, 2013, wherever you buy Harlequin® Blaze® books.

Heaven help her...

Willow Portis tries extra hard to be the good girl of Sweetheart, South Carolina. But the night of the Fall Masquerade, she steps out of her well-behaved shoes and into a supersexy angel costume. And when she's tempted by a stranger, she gives in! Too bad she doesn't recognize her devil until it's too late...

Pick up

The Devil She Knows

by *Kira Sinclair,*

available August 20, 2013,

wherever you buy Harlequin Blaze books.

Red-Hot Reads
www.Harlequin.com